"We're all not quite as sane as we pretend to be."

— *Robert Bloch, Psycho*

CW01499377

BLOOD LANES

Brian G. Berry

Copyright © 2021 Brian G. Berry

All rights reserved

The characters and events portrayed in this book are fictitious. Any similarity to real persons, living or dead, is coincidental and not intended by the author.

No part of this book may be reproduced, or stored in a retrieval system, or transmitted in any form or by any means, electronic, mechanical, photocopying, recording, or otherwise, without express written permission of the publisher.

ISBN-13: 9798474063867
ISBN-10: 1477123456

Cover design by: jorgeiracheta
Library of Congress Control Number: 2018675309
Printed in the United States of America

CONTENTS

PROLOGUE

"What do you think?"

"About what?"

"*About what?* About that asshole back there."

A young face, pitted from a lifetime of acne turned back, small gray eyes beneath a thinning hairline, peered through the wire mesh portal. A man sat gloomed in a shade of black, randomly slashed with the yellow glow of street lamps flashing past. "I don't know—but I'm happy he's back *there*, and I'm up *here*. They should have given him the chair—don't know why we're bringing him up to the hospital."

"It's a *sanitarium,* numb nuts, besides, we ain't paid to think about such things." The rotund man seated behind the wheel took a final drag, blowing two thin streamers of smoke down the front of his indigo blouse which stressed against his belly, the buttons of which were only a couple of pounds of pressure away from springing off and hitting the windshield. He tossed the butt out the window into the street. "I'm hungry, what about you?"

"You're always hungry—we go through this every time we transport."

"Yeah, well, I can't help it."

"Didn't you bring something to eat this time— you know we have quite a drive ahead of us."

"Yeah, I brought some crap along for the ride, but..." the older man, shaped like a septic tank, reached a thick hand that looked more like a bloated pack of hot dogs ready to split, down beneath the seat, hoping to brush along something that would help curb a famished feeling he had bubbling in his gut. "*Fuck*, I thought I had an extra pack of jerky down here—"

"Jimmy, watch out!"

Jimmy jerked the wheel to the left.

"You almost hit that car!" Cray shouted, hooking a thumb out the window.

"Stop your belly aching, kid, this ain't my first transport."

"Yeah, well, you keep driving like an idiot, and it will *both* be our last."

Dragging the wheel to the right, he eased around the last corner that would take them to the highway. "You know something, Cray, you worry too damn much."

"Do I?"

"Hell yes you do! You ever think about relaxing kid? Hell, when's the last time you had any fun, or a mouthful of pussy, huh? Can you answer that?"

Funny question coming from a man who probably hadn't felt something warm in his hands besides that stunted mushroom he called a dick. "I got laid the other night."

"Bullshit!"

"I did!"

Jimmy's corpulent belly rolled with laughter. "Oh yeah? How much she cost?"

"What do you mean?"

Jimmy laughed. "Goddamn kid, you are one clueless sonofabitch."

Cray stared blankly over at his partner.

Jimmy just looked at the kid like maybe he had something wrong with him. "A *hooker* right? You bought a goddamn hooker?"

"Oh...*No*, why the hell would I do that when I have a girlfriend?"

Jimmy rolled his eyes, still thinking about something salty to fill his mouth with. "Yeah, well, whatever, I still don't believe you."

They drove on for another ten minutes, this time in silence, and the quiet agitated Jimmy who loved to talk, who love to hear himself speak. Time wasted transporting a prisoner with no conversation was like pulling on your dick without a magazine paged in tits and pussy to glance over. And that big ugly sonofabitch hunched in the glow of street lights unseated his nerves a bit; ugly on account of the scars running over his face like a topography chart. He knew about the man. Skimmed his record before shackling his wrists tight.

Just another sadistic body stacker.

A man who liked to get his hands bloody. And he wasn't your typical butcher knife cutting madman neither; nor was he the grim silhouette with the double headed axe raised above his head over some screaming teen in the woods. The man liked to break bodies on whatever he could get his hands on, and if he had to use a knife or a hatchet to do it, then good for him.

Headed up state, charged with the brutal massacre over in Venice Beach the week prior, in which he chopped and hacked his way through a bunch of drunken teens during a birthday party. The official count was hard for investigators to determine, being as most of the kids remains were spread out over a couple of blocks of sea front condos, even pieces floating in the surf; scattered over the beach by night waves breaking over the warm white sands.

They say he used a portable boat motor; made fine work of several studs by scraping their faces off at the skull. Another implement was a simple paddle of polished lumber, something an old sea hand would have cradled over his hearth, commemorating some extraordinary time in his life. They say Charles Warner busted that paddle over some poor girls head, cracking her head apart until the end broke off, then used the snapped end as a spear of sorts, forcing its splintered end down the throats of a few others. One of the worst pieces he used was that nasty hooked piece of metal known as a gaff hook. Shaped like an over-sized fishing hook, or something Captain Ahab could have put to good use, Charles Warner utilized it instead to snag them kids as they ran away from him. But you see, those kids—drunk like they were, high on things—had been unable to put enough space between themselves and that man, so he reached out with that sharp point and sank its end into their throats, pulling them in, working them over with a few clawing hacks that punched holes in them big enough to shove a beer bottle in.

He was found walking up a street, carrying something in his hand.

Cops tossed a spotlight on him.

Guns came out after what they had seen.

A stringer of heads. A thick band of nylon dock rope running from their mouths, strung down through their throats, the end knotted in his fist. The heads belonged to a family only two homes down from where they found him wandering at. Three of them were young children, the other was an older gal, which they later discovered was the kid's grandmother.

"Would you look at that..." Something caught Jimmy's eye. "Speaking of hookers."

"What—you thinking of picking her up?" Cray joked.

Relieving a scratch somewhere beneath his balls, Jimmy made a curious face that pulled the folds of his fat up in a grimace. "I'm thinking about it."

"Are you *nuts?* We have a *prisoner!*"

"Won't take but a minute—damn, kid, *live* a little," he shouted. "Take it from me, boy: don't take everything so fucking serious." Jimmy eased up on the gas a bit. The huge truck came to a crawl. "Look at that ass."

Cray poked his head forward, trying to get a glimpse of whatever had Jimmy bulking some meat between his thighs. "Ah man, she's *disgusting,* what's wrong with you?"

"Boy you have no damn taste!"

The girl, slant thin, cheeks sunken, hair stringy —dry as withered sidewalk weeds, was standing in a pool of streetlight. She was carrying a small purse on a long looped gold chain. A gray skirt that could have once been white, hid little of the cherry red thong pushed between her sagging ass cheeks. A crop top of pink with a big scarlet heart on the chest. She looked over to Jimmy, gave him a grin of piss—or puke—yellow teeth. Her dark eyes looked plucked from a corpse.

"She's on drugs man, you can't mess with that."

Jimmy rolled out a laugh that had him slapping his knee. "Boy! Shit—it'll only take a second. Now cover me a minute. I'll take her to that corner, behind the service station over there."

Cray looked to where he was pointing. The place looked closed for the night. Being only 8:30, he suspected the place should have been opened; customers pumping gas, lined up inside. In fact, most of the places they had blew by looked closed, except for a couple of diners and a hotel a ways back, this town, Silverside or something, had a strange feeling to it. "I don't know. What if you get caught?"

"Ain't nobody out here, Cray. What the hell did I tell you?"

Cray was trying real hard to think about what he could have told him.

"Damn kid, your mother drop you a few times on that big ol' head of yours—your brain okay in that skull?"

"My mother never dropped me."

Jimmy laughed another bellowing roar that put some red in his cheeks. "Goddamn, Cray, you are one fucked up kid."

With that, Jimmy released his bulk from the cab. Turning to Cray, he had a funny look on his face. "Hey, you got a twenty on you?"

Cray pulled his wallet out, the velcro scratching. "I have two."

Jimmy smiled. "One will do."

Handing him the bill, Cray sealed the wallet. "Hey, what are you going to do with that?"

Jimmy walked away guffawing in more of that howling laughter.

Cray had been sitting, twiddling his thumbs now for a good five minutes, when the headlights in the passenger side mirror broke his trance with a piercing white glow. He leaned forward to get a better look. "What the—"

The next thing he knew there was an explosive crash from behind, then his head was forced onward through the big windshield, his body following him onto the hood. Bits of glass showered the street. Cray would have screamed out his agony if it weren't for the slice of glass curved like an evil grin sheathed in his neck. His blood poured and poured, rolling in a slick oily wave down the hood, dripping and dropping to the pavement, mixing with the vehicles fluids that were steady rolling down the gutter after the crash had forced the truck forward into a parked Datsun.

He never saw the big midnight blue truck that looked more like a re-purposed package delivery vehicle curbed alongside the road.

With the bottle plugged in his mouth, its bottom scraping the ceiling of his goblin green Viero, he had little time to avoid smacking into the rear of the double door cargo looking truck. But Wade was lucky. He had been wearing his seatbelt. Unlike Cray, who would lay sprawled across the hood of the transport, his face powdered white from a fountaining pour of blood spurting and spraying from his neck.

"Oh, baby, keep sucking it, I haven't felt a tongue this good in years—" A loud crashing noise grabbed his attention away from the tongue coiling over his pathetic meat. "What in the Christ was that!"

The hooker looked up, about to ask a question. "Huh—uuggh"

Jimmy plugged it deeper into her mouth—what

there was of it that is. "Don't worry about it hun, I'm sure it was nothing."

Wade fell from his seat once he pushed the door open.

The bottle, too, went bouncing and rolling into the gutter. "Oh, my fucking head, man..."

He managed to stand. Fixing his silver tie that hung over his shoulder, rubbing his hands over his black suit, correcting any blemishes, of which there were little. Blinking his eyes through a cloud of booze, he saw the damage. "Oh shit, I don't think my insurance is going to like this much." Then he saw the crumpled end of his own car. "*Sonofa-bitch!*"

Moving in a wobble; swaying and catching himself by throwing his hands out, keeping steady to the roof. He saw something moving around near that big truck. "What the fuck is that..."

His eyes were a blur, fogged and glassy, tossing out shapes he couldn't see accurately. What he could make out through a squint was the shadowy like figure emerging from the back of those doors he opened up with the impact.

Somebody was staggering towards him, they moved like they were injured.

"Hey man, you okay? Sorry about the truck, I'm sure my insurance will cover it."

Ignoring the comment, Charles Warner was crouching over something.

There was a crack of glass, like a bottle smashing against a curb.

"If you want to exchange information so I can get on my way, I would be—"

Wade had trouble speaking just then.

The man that tumbled out of those doors was on him, pressed against him. A cracked bottle in his hand. He drove its saw toothed ridges into Wade's face. Blood instantly started pushing from the skin, curdling from the bone like pencil shavings; razored edged teeth biting into the milky white of his bulging eyes. He started choking and thrashing around at the intense pain that literally stabbed and twisted just above his lips.

Grinding the jagged edges deeper into Wade's face, Charles Warner was grunting with the effort, blood was shooting up at him, spraying over the scars on his face, but, eventually, he managed to push it real deep, blowing by pieces of skin, bone, and skull, coring poor drunken Wade's face like an apple.

Wade lay slumped against his own car while Warner tried to pull the bottle loose, but it had embedded itself in deep. Instead, he watched on as a grisly fountain of blood and fluid poured from the neck of the bottle, down the man's chest, flowing and sputtering like a loose spigot.

"Holy shit!" Jimmy wanted to shout it, but it came out as more of a strangled whisper.

The hooker, Tabatha, or some shit, Jimmy couldn't remember, saw the big man out there, and what he had done to that other man, and how a whole bunch of blood pumped from that bottle pushed into his face. She screamed and took off somewhere in the dark. Jimmy didn't bother calling after her, he figured if he could keep quiet, he might make it out of this alive.

He was watching Warner real close. Sticking low and squatting behind an old Plymouth that had seen better days.

Warner was moving to the front of the truck.

"Oh, Goddamn, kid, why weren't you wearing your belt!" He hadn't noticed Cray spread on the hood, covered in glass, and blood. Not until Warner had stood over him.

He was still cuffed, both hands in front of him, as he throw open the door to the truck. He ducked inside, Cray's body was shifting around like Warner was looking for something on his lower half. A second later Warner emerged, tossing the cuffs into the road. He had something else in his hand, but Jimmy couldn't make it out.

And like a shadow, Warner was no more.

Just up and gone, slipping into the night.

Jimmy was relieved.

But the relief was short lived, when, a few moment later, Warner came up behind him. Jimmy shrieked like a swine, his pants unscrolling from his waist, keeping him from running away.

Warner was raising something above him, but Jimmy still couldn't see because he was turned away, doing his utmost to hobble the hell out of there like one of those pillow sack races.

Then Jimmy felt a bludgeoning crack shatter over his skull, the reverberation traveling down his body, exploding from his toes. He dropped, limp as the dick between his legs. A moan blew from his throat that sounded confused, grim, and at a loss to the sudden agony blistering his nerves apart.

Warner brought the nightstick up again, dropping the black polished lumber down into the crown of that fat man at his feet. There was a wet crack that Warner felt in his boots. He raised it again, then came down harder. Jimmy's head split apart. Another blow opened it wider, until finally it spread out in a wide shimmering pool of blood, skull chips, and brain jelly. It stuck to the nightstick, pieces of scalp flaking from it, wisps of bloody hair blowing in the wind.

Warner continued to drop a few more blows into the pile of pulp, until finally he stalked away, disappearing into the cold black night.

CHAPTER 1

"We close in five, but that don't mean none of you leave, you hear me?" Mister Peter Swallecki was a bowl of a man, round as a gluttonous man could get. Big bushy eyebrows that hung low over his copper brown eyes, one of those crawling caterpillar mustaches that obscured his lips. His face was round, his head gleaming off the neon tubing running behind him on the wall. He had a curious look about him that made you think he could have been the mascot for the place. Proportioned like something you would see ambling across your television screen in a cartoon show: Bowling pin shaped, and that head surely resembled a twenty-five pound bowling ball, and just as slick.

"We have some important people stopping by early tomorrow morning and I need this place to shine!"

"Like that fat head of yours?" Stanley Reid commented under his breath, eliciting a few laughs near him.

Peter Swallecki continued. "Now look folks, I know you would rather be clocking out for the night, but I need your help, I can't do this crap by myself—"

"Yeah, no shit." Stanley whispered again.

But this time he said it a bit louder, and Peter looked at him, pausing mid-speech, but then shrugged it off, clearing his throat. "We're a team here at Silverside Lanes, and I expect each and every one of you to act your part."

Everybody in the small crowd gave each other a look, one of those looks like they didn't really want to be there, and enough emotion expressed in those looks that said they had plans tonight, and how could this fat sonofabitch throw a dent into their evening.

"Mr. Swallecki, sir? I can't stay tonight, I have to pick up my kid."

Peter wiped some beads of perspiration from his brow. "And where's your kid, Dianne?"

"With her grandmother, but she can't stay there —"

"Tell your mom to expect a sleepover then, I need all the help I can get, and considering you're on the payroll, you'll be putting in work like the rest of us around here." He looked out into the crowd. "Nobody is exempt from tonight." Then he smiled, that mustache pulled up revealing a set of badly neglected yellow teeth. "Consider it *mandatory*."

There was a unified sigh of bullshit ringing over the crowd.

"That's not fair!"

"What a hardass!"

"Me and Jeremy were planning on seeing a movie—"

"Save it people, I had plans, too—you think I wanted to stay around with you folks? Look, I'll let each of you call whoever you need to call, but then I need you guys to focus and get this done. The quicker we finish here, the faster we get home. And, oh, before I forget, I'm bolstering the roll call with two others from the morning shift, so that should help a bit. So start cleaning what you see, and I'll be back with the task sheets."

Silverside Lanes, the oldest bowling alley in the town of the same name. Erected in the mid 60s, Silverside Lanes was the place to be for the majority of town. That is until the town expanded, blowing up into other things to do other than burning money at the lanes and its stocked tavern.

There was competition in the works.

A few blocks down, the bricks were laid out, stacking everyday and nearly complete. The bosses at Silverside figure it's just a matter of time before they go belly up. The new establishment was said to have three dozen lanes in the plans, compared to Silverside's twelve. There were rumors of not only a tavern, but a bar and grill, a full blown arcade, even a dance floor. The place had no name yet, but everybody at Silverside was calling it *Killer Lanes*, on account it would soon cause them all to be unemployed; and considering most of the workers at Silverside had tried to reach out to the owners of the new place for possible employment, they were told they already had a full crew on hand.

Shit out of luck.

Silverside itself, though not as exquisite as the new place was shaping to be, it did have its attractions, though few as they were. There was a line of arcades strung past the entry, most of them older, but there was a couple of modern ones slotted in there, and it seemed like the kids, even some of the crew, couldn't get enough of those glittering lights and synthesized tracks. They had a new rack of bowling shoes, also a shop to repair cracked and damaged balls. The ball returns were new, less than a year old anyhow, and they returned the balls much quicker than the last belts provided, which sounded scratchy and worn, and took *'too goddamn long'* from many of the complaints noted. Neon tubing ran the perimeter of the place, even on the outside, some of it in zagging lines, either vertical or horizontal; some of the glass tubes were even blown into shapes: triangles, circles, squares. The place had that very modern feel to it the 80s had recently exploded with. There was an old juke box that been flooded with more recognizable bands and groups, ejecting most of the originals from it, boxing them up and stuffing them in the warehouse out back. The place was situated in a wide lot that had little to surround it except an open field to the rear, and to the right—down a ways—was a strip of old buildings, quick going to hell like the rest of the original shops and businesses, making room for the new. One of the newest developments was the Albertsons about a block west of Silverside, which had been thrown up after they flattened Sunnyside Market a few months back. Luckily, Silverside was still surviving regardless of the push against the town populating the area with a more modern feel. Loyalists still held to their traditional holes, and that's what made up the majority of its clients. And tomorrow would be the ultimate say in the place. If it survived, or its owners decided to sell, it was up in the air, and Mr. Peter Swallecki deemed it a priority to get the place looking new again.

"I need everybody up at the front desk, now," Swallecki said over the digital speaker system running through the place. "I'll be handing out assignments."

More grunts rose from the employees. Also a bit of cursing and middle fingers thrown up to the speakers.

"This is bullshit," Stanley bitched. "I cannot *believe* that fucking cow is keeping us here all night for this crap."

"He's just trying to save our jobs, that's how I'm looking at it anyways," Allen told him.

"That prick don't care about our jobs, he cares about looking good and nothing else. If they told him *he* would have a job after this place collapses, then he wouldn't be worrying about keeping *us* here; hell, he'd probably wouldn't give a shit what we did."

Allen just shrugged his shoulders.

The crew was pushing in like mindless undead in a wave of whispered things and grunts of annoyance.

Dianne Wells looked positively defeated as all hell she wasn't let free to go pick up her daughter. Black eyeliner looked like wet coal smudged around her normally blue eyes that belied her twenty-eight years, making her look a decade older. Her apple red hair was lying in a straight sheet down her back, small bangs curled just above those sad looking eyes of hers. Freckles dusted her face. Her narrow cheeks accentuated her petite frame. Long neck. She was dressed in a white colored polo, courtesy of the company. Over the left breast, just above a small pocket, was the logo: a group of bowling pins being blown by the impact of a red ball, Silverside Lanes scratched in a neon pink and purple above that. Covering her thin legs were a pair of rough black jeans, and on her feet were some white sneakers. She was standing there with her arms crossed over her small chest, and her foot tapping impatiently.

Standing near her was Stanley Reid. He was mumbling something about how he had to wait on Mr. Swallecki and he didn't like waiting for Mr. Swallecki. A few years shy of forty, he was running a hand through a thick mop of walnut waves atop his head. He looked over the crowd, making a few faces. His eyes matched his hair, his sockets sunk in a bit. Big nose which jutted and caused many jokes on his account. Thin and lanky, he always had something smart ass to say about anything. And he was the brunt of many complaints registered by customers. Most thought it strange that Swallecki kept him on the payroll. They figured it was because he had once been a good employee so long ago. He was outfitted in an oily smeared red short sleeve, and a pair of sandy colored shorts.

Jeremy Mason and Allen Bowin, were chatting it up, waiting on Swallecki to Humpty Dumpty his ass from the office so they could get their assignments. They were talking about the movie they were sure to miss tonight and how it kind of irritated them, but at the same time they welcomed the extra money, and who couldn't use that? The movie though, it was supposed to be something, and it was only playing tonight, and one other night when they were *both* scheduled for a shift.

The Ravenous Blood Beasts From the Planet Death.

Something about a group of space faring explorers has a malfunction which causes them to land on a little habitable rock in one of the more unexplored regions. They put out a distress call upon landing, where upon they find the atmosphere surprisingly compatible with their lungs, after which they set upon the surface, doing a little... well, exploring, and suddenly, they start getting picked off one by one by these mutated looking horrors, and, well, that's pretty much what the trailer showed them. And being the types who loved trashy films like those, they couldn't wait to check it out. Of course Swallecki had other plans, and it didn't involve much of anything fun.

"How long you think this will take?" Jeremy asked him. Dressed in a blue shirt, sky-blue jeans, black shoes. His hair was thick and wavy similar to Stanley's, only blond. Tall and narrow, he wasn't much to look at, but he didn't mind. His love was cinema and videogames. Pushing twenty-five, he still lived with his parents, on account he was knocking out some schooling, hoping to relieve himself from this crumbling town.

"Not sure, but hopefully not all night, we might still be able to catch the show, or at least most of it. It doesn't start until 11, so we might be done by then." Allen Bowin was the opposite of his friend Jeremy, not in similarities they shared in movies, comics, videogames, and science fiction, but appearance. Around the same age, Allen was slightly bulged around his waist. His cheeks were ballooned out a bit. He had curly dark hair and a thick pair of spectacles that enhanced his green eyes to the size of marbles. He had a company polo stretched across his belly, a gray color. Black jeans ending at red striped white sneakers.

Pauly was walking in from the tavern. Dressed in a red plaid button down, sleeves down to his wrists. Bristles poking from his sun baked face. A short crop of gray and black sat squared on his scalp; a reflection of his old army days. Dark blue jeans and black boots. He had a rag in his hand that was currently wiping away something offending on his knuckles. "Hey, guys," he said sullenly. An older man; been with the place longer than those spread out in front of him. "What's this bullshit we gotta' do some extra work tonight? I wasn't here earlier when Swallecki was running his mouth."

"Oh, he wants this place to shine and be all pretty for the owners who are supposed to show up tomorrow," Stanley injected. "You know how he is."

Pauly rolled his eyes. "Anybody know how long this will take?"

"Consider your nights scrubbed…" a voice said behind him. "We have allot of work to do." Swallecki was waddling over to the crew assembled.

"Come on, Peter, you know I gotta' be out of this place at nine sharp for my wife," Pauly said to him with a flat voice.

"Sorry, Pauly, you can give her a ring, but it's going to be a late one tonight I'm afraid."

Pauly balled up the rag, shoving it in his pocket, joining the others. "This is some bullshit, Peter— you can't be doing this on no notice."

"It's *Mr. Swallecki*, and yes—I can do this. It's in my job description." He pointed at the bronze name plate on his orange polo, which gave him a real pumpkin like appearance.

Pauly looked like he maybe wanted to squeeze some grease out of those folds that ran around Peter like stacks of creamy dough. "Better not eat up my night, that's all I'm saying."

Dismissing Pauly further, Swallecki looked

around. "Where the hell is Hardy?" He was refer- ring to their general fix-it man, Hardy Collins. His place was behind the scenes, fixing all the shit that happened to brake down or apart regularly around the place.

Stanley was the first to speak. "Where do you think?"

He could only be in one place, and that was the storage room, warehouse. A place that smelled of machine parts and oil, workbenches and dirty rags. It was the place that Hardy used to fix all the shit that went wrong. Also, a place that held extra bowling pins freshly painted in racks, bowling balls lined up and ready to replace ones that crack; gears, belts, tools; if it had a place in the lanes, you could be sure to find it somewhere in that junk heap of the storage room.

"Can someone go and fetch him for me?"

"I'll go," Stanley said.

"Go then, and hurry up—no messing around!"

"Yeah, yeah, don't lose your panties."

It took only a moment for Stanley to race off down past the lanes. There was a door set near lane one that opened into the backroom.

Deeply tanned, Hardy had tattoos running up and down his arms; some on his legs. Mostly rock bands and skulls. Headphones cupped over his long black hair that he never seemed to wash that permeated with the same odors as the stor- age room: oily and mechanical. His face was a pit of old acne scars he had as a teen, now in his late 30s, those memories stayed with him. He was drumming his hands with a couple of torque wrenches, smacking over the small table set in the middle of the room, covered in oil and empty cups and rags and bolts. Dressed in an over sized black shirt, a picture of a screaming skull centered in the middle, black shorts that ran past his knees a bit, and a pair of army boots he bought out at the local army/navy surplus, he didn't even notice Stanley running up to him.

"Hardy!"

"Hey, brother, what do you want? Something need fixing?"

"Nah, nothing like that. Swallecki needs us all up front."

Hardy pulled his headphones down from around his neck. "What the hell for?"

"He's making us stay on shift, cleaning and shit like that."

"I'm supposed to be outta' here in…hell, ten minutes ago!"

"Just like the rest of us!"

"*Goddamnit!*"

With that, Hardy followed Stanley out of storage, and back up front. Both of them bitching about Swallecki and the night ahead.

"Nice to see you join us, Hardy—thank you, Stanley."

They both flipped him off as his head dropped down to the clipboard in his pudgy hands.

"Okay, let's see here. *Dianne*, I need you to stick

to the front counter. Make sure all the shoes are properly aligned and free of scuff marks. Also, make sure the laces are inside, I don't want to see any strings loose, okay?"

She nodded her head.

"Also, make sure the counters are gleaming— no stains, nothing. I need it fresh. Anything behind the counter needs arranged and neat looking. When you're done with all that, come see me."

She resigned herself to the night ahead. "Yes, sir."

Flipping to another sheet. "Next, we have *Jeremy*. I need you to spit shine those arcade cabinets over there. Get all those crumbly finger stains off and around those buttons and toggles. Hit every inch of those things, you hear me? After that, I want you to run the vacuum over every square foot of carpet in the place."

Jeremy looked to the orange and purple pattern below him, cartoon images of bowling balls and pins stitched within. "Anything else?"

"Actually, yes, after the arcades, before the carpets, I want you to start in the bathrooms, make 'em shine!"

Jeremy looked over to Allen, shook his head, then back to Swallecki. "Will do."

"*Allen*, I need you to start on the lanes, run the polisher, make sure it's a new pad and make those lanes of lumber shimmer under the glow. I want to see my face in those lanes."

Stanley made a comment under his breath that

Hardy laughed at.

"*Stanley*, seeing that you're enjoying yourself, I want you to polish every ball in the place. Also, the ball returns, and help Allen out with the lanes. I'm expecting perfection and nothing more from you two."

Stanley moaned. "Ah come on, Peter, got anything lighter for me?"

Ignoring him, Swallecki continued to the next sheet of paper. "*Hardy*," he paused a moment. "Clean up that storage room. Make it presentable and please do it thoroughly, I don't want Mr. Henderson to step in a puddle of grease, you hear me?"

Hardy was pumping his head up and down to some notes in his head. "Yea, sure thing, man."

"Now, that leaves... *Pauly*."

Pauly, being older than Swallecki by a good ten years, pushing 56, looked at his boss with a seething eye. "What do you got me doing, Peter?"

"I...just need you to clean up the tavern, make it look new. Nothing more; pretty simple."

Swallecki turned to the rest of the crew. "Now, everybody listen: I need you all to perform these tasks like your jobs depend on it, because honestly they do. We're looking to keep this place open, but that's up to the big boss, so let's show him that we take great care of this place, and how we still bring in a good portion of the town, and not let them draw a conclusion that we're being lazy over here, okay?"

A few grunts mumbled out.

"*Also*, when you are finished with your assignments, please come to me so I can inspect your work, and when I deem you finished, you can help whoever is lagging behind, you hear me?"

There was a lot of bickering after that.

About how someone could take advantage of that, and how they could lounge back and wait for help so as not to put out any effort.

"There will be none of that," Swallecki told them. "If I catch anybody lazing on their task, I will *fire* you on the spot! This is no time to be selfish. You hear me?"

The crowd started to disperse, more heated grunts coming from whispered lips. "*Oh!* One other thing, I pulled two more from the morning crew, they should be showing up any minute now to help y'all out."

"Who'd you get?" Stanley wanted to know.

Swallecki licked his lips. "Maxine Macy and Jo-anne Phillips."

Stanley let out a whooping wail. "Oooh boy, Maxine? Good choice, Swallecki!"

"That's *Mr. Swallecki*, Stanley. And no messing around, you hear me?"

With that, everybody had broke apart. Each going to their own corners. The mood was sour, unpleasant, but the night ahead was sure to bring something allot worse, something born in the darkest of nightmares.

CHAPTER 2

"Damn, it's getting cold out here, brother." The sinking of the sun had brought with it a chilling cold to settle into their bones. What was hours ago a nice warm day was sucked away with a gale of glacial drifts blowing down the alley they called home. Silverside was funny like that, even in the dwindling days of September, the night could bring a wintry feel whenever the sun was finished bringing life to things.

"Sure is, but thankfully we got this," Frank said, dragging out a corked bottle of something that was sure to warm their bodies over.

Martin, blowing heat in the palms of his hands cupped over his mouth, looked past the flames licking out of the barrel at his feet. "Oh, the *good* stuff. Where'd you get it?"

Frank told him how he slipped into the Korner Mart, and when Jerry, the owner, was fighting with some obnoxious bastard, he went about pulling it from the shelf, pocketing it, and getting the hell out of there before Jerry caught him.

"Good, good. I haven't had a nip all day."

A hollow pop was heard as the cork was twisted

free. The bottle upended, plugged between Frank's lips. Flames in the fire barrel were reflecting off the glass. "Ahhhhh, now *that* is some good shit. Here."

Martin grabbed at the bottle proffered to him over the flames. Holding it up. "Cheers." He took a generous pull. The liquid pumped down his throat, pooling in his belly. "I needed that, *oh boy*, did I need that!"

There was movement approaching. A man was there.

Darrel had just woken up. He had a long day behind him. While his friends sat around collecting shit to burn for the night, he had been out working some bullshit job that paid ten bucks, which he later used to buy a burger over at the Grease Shack. After, he hit the Korner Mart and blew the rest on a few 40oz barrel bottles that he ending up pissing out after finishing. He passed out after that, couldn't remember where, but it was far from home.

He smelled the fire pushing at him from down the block, knew it had to be Frank and Martin. "Hey guys." Darrel's voice was slurred, sleepy, hollow and scratchy. Dehydrated.

"Where the hell you've been at?" Martin asked him, his hands poised over the flames. His long woolen coat flapping from a wind gust threading the alley. An old dirty ball cap hid his long brown hair, a face weathered by years of harsh living. "We were wondering if we would see you tonight."

Darrel strolled up to the firelight. Hands outstretched ahead of him, going for the heat. A fat bulging blue windbreaker concealed his slim frame. Knotted short hair lay frozen to his scalp. Dirt smudged his face from where he wiped his brow during the day. "Doing work for Scott again."

Frank finished a long pull. "He pay you today?"

"Nah..." he lied.

"Damn." The bottle sloshed its contents again. Frank pushed it out to him. "Take this, warm you up a bit."

Darrel took the bottle, slugged down a pour. "*Whew!* Good and strong."

The bottle was passed around until there was little left besides the ring of backwash that accumulated. Laughter bellowed down the alley, voices high in booze; loud and boisterous, filled the space. The barrel was fed a steady helping of old lumber, boxes, broken furniture pieces; whatever they could get their hands on that would burn. Wind continued to blow around and scatter loose debris, whipping it into the crevices and small spaces between the dark buildings that loomed against a blacker night. The moon overhead watched them, a bleached eye driven in a scintillating mass of glittering points.

He could hear them down there.

Voices.

At least three from the sounds of it. Loud and full of intoxication. The wind was carrying the smell to him. He needed more blood. To feel its warm grease on his hands.

At the alley mouth, he looked around; there had to be something laying about that he could use. His eyes fell upon something just then. He scooped it up, and started down the alley.

"I think it's a perfect plan!" Frank slurred. "You distract him; I'll swing in after that, and snatch two or three bottles this time. And if he catches us, we push him down, take what we want, pull his phone from the wall!" His laughing resounded down the alley, echoing—bouncing—between the walls.

Frank's plan sounded good to them.

With the bottle since dropped in the barrel, they were listing and swaying from the high. It felt good; the cold all but forgotten as it continued to trail into the alley. Their bones were warm, their skin still cold, but they couldn't know, not with the booze swimming, lapping the walls of their bellies. Their faces were slack and restless, eyes glassy balls of wetness; silver looking from the flames.

"You think it'll work?" Martin asked Frank.

"I know it will. That old coot is a moron, we'll get what we need."

Darrel was blowing heat in his hands, rubbing it on his face. "Hey, who's that over there?"

Frank and Martin followed his eyes.

There was a man coming down the alley. A big shadow of a man.

"Mikey, is that you?" The outline looked like

their old friend, Mikey. They hadn't seen him since he went missing a ways back.

"That ain't Mikey," Martin said. "He ain't moving around like Mikey anyhow."

That was true. Mikey had a strange gait to his movements; a dragging like shamble, a product of his time running around on the other side of the world for the government in those hot jungles. Whoever that was coming down the alley was moving with a confidence. Strong, and...something else they couldn't quite put to it.

"Can I help you friend?" Darrel called out to the stranger.

The man stopped. A black shadow. Feet apart. A silhouette of a man, hidden; tucked away by the darkness outside the circle of light at their feet.

They watched him, standing over there, no longer moving.

"Something we can do for you fella?"

Then the man moved, not his whole body, just his arm, like he was pitching something from his hand.

The sound was an atrocious note that went up both men's spines. The brick thudded onto the ground after it smacked Darrel in the forehead. Darrel folded up, dropped to the ground like the sack of proverbial bricks after that. Blood seeped from the gash that opened up his head, misting off the pavement.

Frank and Martin stood shocked. Mouths open, watching all that blood come sludging out of the wound that looked more like a hatchet strike.

Movement tore them away from the blood. That man was moving out there, heading towards them.

Still frozen, they watched as he came near.

The firelight threw aspect to him, brought his features alive. And it scared them. Not just what he had done, though that put a few grays in their scalp, it was the look of the man. Those ugly scars that looked like knife slashes cut across his face. Bristles poking from his head, probably a week of growth, and no more. His skin was dark, tanned from living beneath the sun for too long. He was wearing some sort of workman's outfit. A one piece, like a flight suit. Gray, long sleeves, a zipper right up the middle. It did little to guess at the muscle beneath. His frame was powerful, corded— deadly.

The brick found his hand again. He looked at the two standing only a foot away. Their faces were screwed up in horror, their hands out in front of them, warding him away. He looked back down to the man that was bleeding. Swinging the brick back down onto the man, he flattened out his skull until it cracked apart, blown into fragments; blood flooded, carrying pieces of skull with it; the sound of it leaking down the storm drain a few feet away sounded awful to their ears.

Tossing the brick aside. He threw out his arms, grabbed Frank by the shoulders who snapped from the fugue, started hollering for help and screaming.

Warner cracked him across the face with a solid fist that was more like a ball of tungsten steel.

Frank went slack, limbs limp.

Warner pushed the man's head into the barrel. The flames instantly crawled up the man's scalp. His hair made that sizzling cracking sound, black smoke rose into the night. Then the rest of his body was forced deeper into the barrel. But it was becoming troublesome for Warner because the body wasn't responding like he had hoped. Instead, he shoved, folded, and forced that man into the barrel. The flames did good work, licking over him. The old jean coat he wore quickly fell to the heat, burning up from all the oil it had soaked up over the years working odd jobs as a mechanic. Next, the pants turned to flakes of black ash. His skin started sputtering and popping, blistering, blood was congealing and boiling like burnt sugar. The flesh on his face ran down his head like tallow, melting away; his skull was smiling out from the flames as his lips shriveled up like dying worms.

Warner was standing over the barrel, watching all this with a manic gleam in his black eyes.

Martin started screaming, turned and ran.

Warner watched him go, running down the alley, the man's coat billowing behind him, his ball cap coming off his head, the sound of his cries spearing into the night.

Martin was running. Where he was running to,

he couldn't be sure. All that was driving him away was the image of that man somewhere behind him in the alley. *Is he following me?* It was hard to tell. There were noises around him. Mostly the wind. But there were scattering sounds, too.

He had ran out of the alley, headed into town. *Maybe somebody can help me. Flag down a cop or something.*

But so far he hadn't seen a single person yet. The town was dead. Normally traffic was something you would see, considering it was Friday. But he also knew this side of town was pretty much for the dead, or at least *soon* to be dead. The old businesses that once flourished have since surrendered to the worm. Folks were closing up shop. Buildings looked more like mausoleums and tombstones jutting from the cold earth, collecting weeds and cobwebs.

There was a set of headlights poking through the dark, coming at him.

He started limping towards the street. Out in the distance he could see that bowling alley that once told him to stay away from the dumpsters.

The lights were still on inside. The pinkish haze of neon stripping that wrapped around the place, scattered some of the night away. Way above the entrance was that image he had seen many times, bleating out like a signal at sea: a bowling ball lined in red, smacking a series of white pins. Above it, glowing in neon tubing like the rest, was the name: Silverside Lanes.

The headlights were close.

He ran out into the street. "Help! Help me plea —"

A hand sealed over his mouth.

His feet left the ground.

He was pulled away back into the shadows of an awning.

The car swept by, making a left down the winding strip of road that led out of town.

Warner watched as the car drove away.

Turning the man to face him.

Martin screamed.

Warner swung his arm overhead, cracking Martin on the skull. His body went to rubber.

Placing the man on the cold ground, Warner fixed his jaw to the curb. There was a cracking sound in his mouth, like bone and muscle splintering, after forcing the man's teeth to hold to the concrete. Warner made a grunting like noise as he reared back, dropped a heavy foot into the man's skull. His head blew apart, the back of his head buckling, folding in half; the sound blew into the night like a lone gunshot.

He kicked the man over to examine his work.

Blood and teeth lined the gutter. His mouth pulled wide, comically wide. His jaw hung loose and pathetic, detached from his upper plate. His tongue looked phallic, hanging limp and wet, coated in blood. His eyes were wide, as though he still lived, but there was no life in those eyes, only two dark pinpoints for pupils.

A cold wind threw a shiver over him as he stood looking at the mess.

Then a light caught his eye.

A short walk away was a bowling alley.

There was movement in the parking lot. Two girls, from the looks of it, were making their way to the front of the place, huddled together to fight the cold. He could hear them giggling even from the distance that separated them.

He grunted in his throat as his feet smacked over the pavement in a sticky mess, heading for those lanes, where the blood would really start to flow.

CHAPTER 3

Dianne Wells brushed back the strands of red hairs that had fallen past her shoulder after placing another pair of well polished shoes back in their spot.

Only another hundred to go!

She grabbed another pair, dabbed the squat brush in her hand with another creamy layer of brown polish, she started to wipe at the tips of the shoes on the counter in front of her. Swallecki already warned her once not to be doing that over the counter top, said it could leave a stain, but right then she didn't give a flying fuck what he thought or wanted.

You see, Dianne was pissed off. She should have been home with her daughter, not spreading polish on some old crusty shoes that smelled damn horrible.

Each day she came to work she felt the same: sullen, depressed, done with everything. There was nothing here for her anymore. *It was supposed to be a summer job*, she would tell herself. Of course that was five summers ago, back when she was in school, back when she felt good about herself. Back when she had Anthony—the love of her life. They had gotten a place together, and shortly after that, Melissa came along.

Their baby.

Their world.

But then something happened to Anthony. At first, the doctors said they didn't know what it was. Said the chances were slim. They said this to her, while she looked over the doctors shoulder, over to Anthony. He was smiling at her; a hopeful kind of smile that he was needing real bad for her to return. But the only thing on her face was a sheet of tears, and those tears wouldn't stop running from her eyes.

It was several months later when she was finally allowed to see her husband, up close. They warned her, said he could be contagious on account of they didn't know just what in the hell they were dealing with. It wasn't cancer or any myriad form of exotic diseases they were aware of. But whatever it was, it was slowly eating away at Anthony. Devouring each cell slowly, and painfully.

They outfitted her in something she had seen in a movie once. One of those big bulky white space looking suits and visor, thick white gloves. The partition was swung aside and the tears came immediately. Not just tears mind you, but screams. They had to hold her back; arms interlocked around her own. Anthony looked scarcely human anymore. Whatever had been running malignant in his bones had nearly ate the skin from his body. He was flattened looking. What skin there was looked gray, and mottled with sores. Unlike scabs, these sores looked more wet, filled with oily, milky juices that slowly oozed from the thin membranous tissue that sealed them. It was his eyes, though, that she would still see in her nightmares: cherry red eyes, like two crystal orbs full of blood. And those eyes followed her around that room as she lashed out at the doctors holding her back; there was still life somewhere holding on in those bloody pools.

Anthony passed the next day. They burnt his body; denied her request to save the ashes—something she could have sitting in her bedroom in a little urn to remind her of the good times. Information later came out saying he had a rare—and in this case more like 'never before seen'—form of aggressive cancer, and left it at that.

Melissa was born shortly after. She tried her hand at continuing school, but found she couldn't concentrate no more. She had to see doctors, therapists, anybody who would listen, but generally still never understood.

She would come awake at night, after the nightmares—horrible fright episodes of her husband coming after her in some dreary woodland setting like a stretched out scarecrow with wet red eyes. Her naked body pushing through a thicket of thorny pines cutting into her flesh, a terrible wind blowing across the night. She would hear Anthony out there, pushing through the brush, somewhere close. His voice was rasping a terrible wheeze, like diseased lungs fighting to push out air. She could feel his poisonous breath on her neck; his screeching cries and howling moans. And each time he wrapped those long bony fingers around her neck, she would shoot up in bed in a feverish sweat, shrieking and screaming. And then Melissa would scream, too.

It had been about a year since she last had one of those. And she thanked God each day that her husband hadn't visited her anymore in her sleep.

"*Dianne!*" Swallecki was making his rounds again, keeping his on eye on folks. "What did I tell you last time? No polishing on the counter!"

"But I have nowhere else to do this!"

"Not my problem; get a chair, find something to work with—just stay off the counters! I'm not warning you again!"

Her jaw tightened. "Yes, sir…"

As he waddled away, her eyes slanted thin as she watched him go. *I should just quit—walk right out of here!* She pressed the pad of polish down on the tip until the bristles smashed outward. *Not like anybody would care, besides, what am I getting out of this job? Each dollar I make goes straight to rent—and my mom.* It still bothered her that her mother asked her for money when she knew her daughter barely irked out a living working the lanes. *I should just grab Melissa, take what money I have left and blow this town, find a new life somewhere else!*

She tossed the pair of shoes below the counter, not worrying about straightening them—or finishing them.

The digital notes and synthesized tracks of the arcade cabinets never got old, and as Jeremy went about with the glass cleaner, misting clouds over each screen, wiping away all those gummy fingerprints and whatnot, he wished he could slot a few coins inside, try his hand right now. *One day I'm going to beat that Ghost & Goblins, you could be sure of that.* Another fine misting spray hit the marquee, the red rag in his hand smoothing away any noticeable blemish.

"*Shit!*"

He turned his head to see where that shout had come from.

Dianne again. She looked disheveled, stressed, and worn out like an old shop rag.

He figured as much. Jeremy learned about what happened to her husband from Allen. It sounded awful, he couldn't imagine living through something like that. He took a deep breath and blew it out. Continued to work over the cabinets.

"Jeremy!"

He turned his head. "What's up?"

It was Allen, he was leaning on the buffer handle out on the lanes, taking a break from the looks of it. He was wiping some sweat off his forehead with the back of his arm. Stanley was a ways down from him, working over the balls with a rag in his hands.

The neon lighting pushed a color palette of pinks and purple blooms over the lanes. It was quite beautiful when you just looked at it for a minute, but after seeing it so many times over the years, it got to where you just stop noticing things like that anymore.

"How are those arcades coming?" Allen shouted at him.

Jeremy was working one of the toggles, using his fingernail to scratch away some old cheese from the stem. "Almost finished with these!"

"Then off to the bathrooms, huh?"

Jeremy nodded his head. "Afraid so."

"You're going to love it in there, Jeremy."

Jeremy turned his head away from Allen, looking over to Stanley. "Why's that?"

He smiled. "Because I just took a giant dump in there. Forgot to flush it. Sorry about that Jeremy," he laughed. "It's pretty big, looks like it might plug up those pipes."

"Oh, thank you so much, Stanley!" *You fucking prick.*

"Sorry, my friend, when you have to go, you have to go!" he laughed some more.

"Well, maybe you should have flushed it after!"

"I was afraid it would come right back up at me," Stanley chuckled. "Besides, I'm sure you'll have no problem working the plunger in there."

Jeremy looked ahead to the arcades, a look of anger on his face. He sprayed another cone of glass cleaner over the screen of a Galaga machine.

"Be careful when you're in there, Jer' it could be alive—might jump out at you!"

Jeremy didn't bother to turn around, instead, he was just listening to Stanley out there in the lanes, laughing, and laughing—growing more pissed off just hearing it.

"Stop messing around out there, Stanley, or it's your ass!" Swallecki said, walking by with that clipboard in his hand. "I don't want to hear anymore banter and shouting coming from the three of you anymore, you hear me?"

"But Mr. Swallecki, sir, I didn't even say anything."

"Can it, Allen! I heard you shouting things over to Jeremy."

Jeremy turned to Swallecki who was walking towards him. "Allen was just asking if I was almost finished is all, sir."

Stopping in front of Jeremy, Swallecki picked at something in his teeth then worked an itch somewhere in the folds of his thighs. Glancing over the arcades, he said, "Looks to me like these need another cleaning."

"But this is my second time going over them," Jeremy said dejectedly.

"Then get started on the third round!"

Swallecki turned around, eyeballing Allen from across the way, Jeremy made a face behind him; started jumping around, imitating him, his arms flailing, acting like he was holding his own clipboard, barking orders, pushing out his stomach, which was considerably difficult for him on account he weighed as much as just one of Swallecki's legs. Allen watched this, and couldn't help laughing.

"What's so damn funny, Allen?"

"Nothing, sir."

"Then get back to work! No more horseplay, you hear me?" Turning to face Stanley down the lanes, he pointed. "And that goes for you, too—no more warnings you guys!"

With that, Swallecki continued his patrol of the place.

"Look at them in there. Bunch of boys, nothing more. They'll never grow up."

Joanne ran another line of strawberry lip balm on her thick bottom lip. Smacking them both together. "How do I look?"

Maxine looked to her friend. Her hair, thick and brushed over in a wave behind her back, was the color of harvest gold. Thick lips that shined with the pink lighting. Eyes of violet lavender. Slender; she looked dressed for a night out rather than helping bolster a cleaning crew. Tight leather black pants that held to her skin, a braided like texture running along each leg. A sleeveless purple top of silk. Over that, a black leather coat patched in numerous bands Maxine hadn't even heard about. *Punk Maggots, Flesh Eaters, Circle of the Worm.* It was all those strange punk bands she knew her friend liked to listen to. She was aware Hardy was the influence here. She loved the guy, but did he love her back? Or just love what she gave him?

"I think you look *hot*."

Strawberry polished lips pulled wide, she leaned in for a hug. "Thanks sweetheart!"

Joanne's perfume stuck to her, it smelled good, *real* good, and its fragrance of showered roses put a chill in Maxine's body. "You *smell* good, too."

Her friend smiled, continuing to run a line across those plump lips again.

Maxine loved Joanne. She would never tell her of course. Being shy as she was, it could never be divulged. Besides, she knew Joanne was gushing over Hardy, she couldn't understand why. *He's almost 40 for Christ sakes*, she would tell her. *You're 26, don't you think that's a little... weird?* Joanne would tell her how it really wasn't all that weird at all, and that they were both in love, and all that bullshit. But Maxine had a few words she wished she could put out there to her. Tell her how she thought about her often. About how she dreamed of her.

"You think he's paying overtime?" Joanne asked her, growing impatient with knocking on the double glass doors that had that god awful metal casing zagging up and down each side like jail bars, a terrible design if you asked her. It was supposed to be a *cool* design of bowling lanes running up to a group of pins blowing out in a strike, but looked like hell, as if the designer hadn't thought about exactly what he was making. It looked more like a strange sun stuck in a cloud, rays of light shining downward, all of it made from thick metal crafts-manship. She removed her fist from in-between one of the 'lanes'. "Where the hell is Swallecki at?"

Maxine peered behind the latticework. "There he is, he's coming."

And he was: waddling like he always did, that clipboard squeezed in his fat hand. His bald head gleaming in a neon film. His pumpkin colored shirt, those smelly looking white shorts he never seemed to part from. Socks resting half way up his shin with a yellow band near the top.

He opened the door. His bald head sticking out. "About time you two show up, I was wondering if you'd make it." He looked over to Maxine, his eyes never leaving her.

Joanne looked annoyed that he wouldn't fully open up. "Can we come *in* now?" she asked with a shake of her head, wondering why he hadn't let them in yet.

Swallecki continued to look right at Maxine. He could feel the excitement warming his crotch over. Swallecki couldn't get over the way her breasts pushed at the blue polo beneath her coat. Her nip-ples were spearing through whatever bra she was wearing. Her hair was pulled back in a thick black ponytail that laid down her right shoulder. Her eyes were big and wide; green and shiny. Thin, but packed just right, her body was a piece. Her blue jeans were tight and revealing, he couldn't wait to see her from behind.

"Yeah, come on in, girls."

Joanne blew right by him like a gust.

Maxine gave him a forced smile and walked past him, a little too close for comfort, like maybe he wanted to feel her body brush over his own.

After the doors sealed and locked behind the two girls, Swallecki let them know just what was going on tonight. He gave them each an assignment that he expected to be performed with the utmost attention to detail, and there was to be absolutely no screwing around, or else...

Joanne pleaded with Swallecki to help Hardy in the backroom, but he was aware of what they had for each other, so that wasn't happening, not on his watch. So she was assigned to assist Pauly and Dianne.

Maxine was to wipe down the scoreboards on each lane, *better to see her ass that way*, he thought. Then after she was finished with that, she could help him organize his office, of course he didn't tell her that just yet... He said it all with a face she didn't like, or find much amusing. She was feeling something strange in his eyes, but she shrugged.

"Is this overtime, Swallecki?" Joanne asked.

"Overtime? Are you nuts? Nobody is being paid overtime."

Joanne looked over to Maxine, then back to Swallecki. "But we already worked 8 hours today!"

"I don't care if you worked ten, nobody is getting overtime, you hear me?"

"Well maybe I don't feel like working then." Joanne said, indignantly.

"It's mandatory, and both of you are working, are we clear?"

Joanne rolled her eyes and walked away, a bit heated.

Maxine followed her, feeling Swallecki's gaze burning over her.

The doors sealed with the click of a lock that echoed over the parking lot.

He could see the fat man in there, both girls walking past him. He was saying something to those girls, waving a clipboard around. Warner wasn't interested in that. He was interested in the blood that was ripe for the harvest. He needed it, craved it, wanted to paint his face with it. Splash it on the walls, play with it. A cold wind kicked across his face. The moon throwing a pale gleam on the black lot. There had to be another way inside, one less conspicuous. He was thinking the place had a back door. He just needed to find it. But first, he needed to get eyes on his prey.

CHAPTER 4

Pauly slugged down another drink that misted his eyes. The booze brought him some solace in the fact that he had to work more than he intended tonight.

Swallecki, that fat prick, he knows my wife needs me home every night to watch over her.

Cynthia Jackson had what most call mental problems, but what they really consisted of were a host of living nightmares that visited her, mostly in the early hours of black that the AM brought with it. She woke up many nights hearing things outside that just weren't there. Voices whispering through the windows, calling out to her. Knocks on the front door—not simple knocks mind you —these were sluggish and deliberate, like the way your heart does, pulsing slowly as you sleep. There were others noises, too, but most she wouldn't describe. It was linked to her childhood. During a late night, her mother at work, her father far removed from her life, ten year old Cynthia was all alone. It was getting around midnight when a knock hit the door. Too afraid to answer it, on account her mommy said to never open that door when she was gone, and to further put some fear in her skin, she would say things like: 'or else the Nightman would take you away from me.' But something compelled Cynthia to peek through the window that night. There was a man outside in a black coat, and he noticed the little girl peeking out at him. He bent over, showing her his yellowing teeth and eyes big and wide, crazed and gleaming. His fist punched through the window, Cynthia screamed as the fingers found her hair, determined to pull her right out that window, until a car came screeching up, blue and red flashers spinning over the block. It was the police. When Cynthia's mom arrived home, they told her he had been spotted in the neighborhood that night, and the man was a known child abductor. It was the real Nightman momma had warned her about, or something far worse.

But who's the Nightman? Cynthia would ask her mother.

'He wears a long black coat, like the reaper—his face is a wall of black, and if he reaches for you, you will scream when you see his fingers are bones!'

Cynthia would reel back as her mother's own fingers curled and clawed towards her, that awful grin on her face.

'And if he takes you from me, you'll go where the rest of the children go.'

Where do they go momma?

Into the cauldron of course—

That's the part where Cynthia usually

screamed.

You could say her mom had a heavy helping with her lifelong phobias, one that gradually got worse with each year, and the man in the heavy woolen black coat that night, only exacerbated those fears to a crippling degree.

Now she lived the life of a recluse, Pauly the sole provider and teacher of things in the world for her. Too afraid to watch TV at times unless she was certain there were easy, comforting, funny things on the tube.

Pauly loved her, loved her very much. But during their long marriage, going on 30 years now, there had been many rough stretches. The pain had been etched into his face over the years, a new wrinkle here, a blemish there. Like a stump of oak rings, lines and age have weathered his looks.

The bottle was his only friend now, after most of the good people in his life had dismissed him outright due to the fact that he was about as free to do things as most prisoners, or a corpse.

And now, pulling chairs from the ground, placing them on the empty tables, he needed another drink right about then.

Behind the bar of polished dark wood, which stretched a good couple of dozen feet, he placed a glass. Two fingers of bourbon sloshed in its cavity. His rough hand wrapped it, tossing his head back, the harsh liquid burned nicely down his throat. Dipping a rag inside, he washed it out, replacing it with the others.

Surrounding him was allot of that pinkish light Swallecki insisted wrap around the place.

He hated it.

A bar should look like a bar. Dark, low light, sheets of tobacco smoke drifting like a roiling fog bank over a nighted moor. Men hunched over, tossing back drinks, discussing their lives, bitching and moaning about how bad those lives were going. Laughter, gratuitous conversation, jokes. The sound of billiard balls crashing, folks arguing over wrongful calls over some green field on the tube. It hadn't been like that since he could remember, not ever since those goddamn lights brought a queer look to the place that he didn't like very much. He even went about cracking a few of those tubes before, but Swallecki found out, told him he would be fired if he ever did some shit like that again.

Running the same rag over the counter top that he used for the glass, he found the remote, aimed it at the small TV bolted above his bar, in the far corner. He pressed the button, a box of static, then a blue glow, then finally what looked like the news came piecing together. Pauly threw up the volume. "—convicted on the massacre of more than a dozen young celebrants during a birthday party taking place along the coast in Venice Beach, including three children and the grandmother of those children, Charles Warner was denied prison, instead, would live out the rest of his days at Hollow Falls Sanitarium, an extension of Blue Ridge

Sanitarium which resides north, up in Washington state—"

"I remember hearing about him."

Pauly turned his head away from the TV.

Joanne Phillips, he couldn't stand the girl. So full of herself. Always putting on that makeup, wearing things with gross named bands and rock groups that he didn't care for. *She would be a real looker if she took the time to present herself like a real lady*, Pauly thought, *but I guess these young girls today only care about music and looks.*

"Did you see those images that leaked?"

Pauly looked right through her when she spoke. "Nah, I don't watch the news much."

Joanne grabbed a chair off one of the tables, placed it a few feet away, tossed her feet up on the freshly cleaned surface. A file running beneath her long red nails. "It was something, man. There were several bodies lined up on a sidewalk, and, man, they were totally butchered to all hell. Whatever he did to them, was definitely gnarly."

"Maybe you shouldn't be liking things like that, it's not good for the soul, young lady."

"Oh come on, Pauly, you fought in the war, you had to have seen some shit like that."

Pauly did see some shit, thank you very much. He saw plenty of it, participated in his fare share of it, too. Men blown apart, storming up hills soaked and muddy with blood, only to be chopped into slabs of smoking meat from some hidden machine gun nest. The coiling trail of a missile loose from a gook rocket in the bush, headed right at you and your squad. Was nothing gnarly or funny about that. It was horror, *real* horror. When you saw the face of a young man, just out of high school, crying and screaming, his expression twisted in terror when the bullets just wouldn't stop smacking the sandbags; drilling the mud walls only a few inches from his scared, shrunken form—you looked at the glorified side of it in a different light.

"Yeah," he said. "I've seen plenty enough of it to turn that powdered face of yours a shade whiter. Why do you wear so much of that clown grease anyways?"

Ignoring his question. The file grinding away something she didn't like. "It would have made a helluva an album cover."

"What would?" He asked perplexed.

"The *bodies*, Pauly, the ones they showed on the news, man!"

You are one sick bitch, someone needs to whoop your ass. "That's disgusting, Joanne."

She continued to file away, blowing on her nails. Her eyes looking over each one.

"What are you doing here anyhow?"

"Swallecki called us in. Said something about he needed help tonight, didn't give me much of a choice of what I had to say in the matter."

"Yeah, he's hoping we all pitch in and get this place in tip top shape."

"It's a dump."

He would agree with her on that point.

"Well, why you just lounging in my bar?"

"He told me to help you and Dianne. She looked pissed off, so I came in here first."

Pauly just looked at her. Those long legs crossed over one another. Her tongue licking over her lips, making some moaning sound.

"Mmmm, Strawberry."

"What's that?" He asked.

"Strawberry gloss on my lips taste so good."

Did she know I was looking at her? "So you just gonna' sit there while I clean over here?"

"What do you want me to do?" She asked, not bothering to look at him.

"I reckon there ain't much you can do in here, maybe roll the carpet sweeper over the floor?"

Still concentrating on her nails. "I can do that."

He pointed. "It's over there in the corner."

She filed for a moment longer before standing up. Slipping off her leather jacket, she placed it on the table after putting the chair back in place. She was braless, her nipples pushing out against the silken top. Pauly had to look away, lest he think shit that would get him in trouble.

The closet door swung open before her. She grabbed up the sweeper, started rolling it over the carpet. The wheels squeaked each time she went up with it. "Damn this thing sounds like shit."

"Yeah, it's pretty old."

She continued to roll around the carpet, her breasts moving with each stroke.

Pauly turned away from her, dusting the bottles

behind the bar, his eyes hitting up at the screen now and again. Hoping for a distraction on the tube.

Swallecki wasn't around, too focused on Maxine over there to worry much about what he was doing. Finished up with the cabinets, Jeremy felt the coins burning in his pocket. Looking around, he slotted a quarter in the Ghost & Goblins cabinet.

The track started immediately. A young knight sitting on a patch of grass with a princess. Above them, a winged demon. It moves in, grabs the girl, takes to the moonlight. Now the knight, fully armored, is ready. The undead sweep towards him. A large lance launches from his hands, pulling the grave crawler apart.

"Ah yeah, I'm going to finally get through this level—I can feel it!"

As he continued to chop and spill his way through the game, what he didn't know was the pair of eyes on him from the doorway just a little ways down.

Those eyes were looking right at Jeremy. Seething. Warner needed to get to that young man in there. Bury his fingers in his throat, pull a wet flap away; listen to the sounds of that bubbling air fighting up his neck. Maybe pull his teeth out; each one jerked from his jaw; Warner could see the blood jetting from each hole plucked of its tooth. Better yet, grab that tongue of his, pull at it until it came loose with a ripping sound that would travel up most folks spine, but not Warner—it was a good sound, a comforting one; brought him a sick joy even.

There were several others moving around, each of them busy with a task. A guy running a buffer over the lanes, looking like he was having a damn hard time of it by the way all that red was flooding his face. There was a girl behind the counter a ways down; shoes in her hands, polishing them or something. Another girl out on the lanes, using a stepping ladder, spraying and wiping the scoreboard screens. That fat guy was behind her, clipboard under his arm, looking right at her. There was one other guy he could see down the lanes a bit, working at the balls with a rag. Even from Warner's distance he could see the guy was spitting on the balls, giving it his own polish.

He needed to get inside.

Time to go around back.

CHAPTER 5

"Get that corner up there, Max, can't leave any surface untouched!"

He was acting like a big mean boss, his words sharp and heavy with the way an attentive boss should be. But inside, wearing him like a sleeve, there was something else, and it was enjoying the way Maxine moved that rag; how her hips swayed side to side with each stroke, the way the bottoms of her breasts bounced. Her blue jeans were tight fitting, slick and slim against her legs like a second skin. Swallecki had to fight his hands away from himself.

"Okay, finished with that one."

Each ass cheek was prominently displayed through the thin material as she lowered herself down the step ladder. Feet on the ground, she spun around, dragging the ladder with her to the next lane.

"Pick it up, Max, I don't want any drag marks on these lanes!"

"Oh, sorry, sorry."

Lifting the ladder, she carried it over, setting it down, propping it open again. *Is he just going to stand there and watch me the whole time?* "Is there anything you need from me?" She asked a bit nervously.

He stood there a moment in silence before answering. *Oh yes, there's plenty I need from you.* As if reading her mind, he countered. "No, that'll be it. Just making sure you three don't start slacking off."

She turned away from him, moving up the ladder. A mist of spray peppered the screen above her. She could see his reflection in it, and didn't like the look of it very much. The clipboard was in front of him, his fingers were worming over the back of the board like fat white maggots slithering around the edges. She sprayed that spot, only to rid herself of thoughts that were quickly taking shape. As she wiped up the chemical splash, she saw that Swallecki was no longer there.

She turned abruptly, thinking he was standing right behind her.

She wouldn't put anything past him. Maxine was well aware of those looks she would get from him every now and again. Something a drooling man would make looking at a foldout in one of those smut magazines full of carnal things. It had been going on since she could remember. It never really bothered her much at first, she was used to men giving her faces, watching her walk, looking at her shapely breasts as they bounced with each step. But this...there was something bad lurking in that face of Swallecki's. Like he had a plan brewing;

a contingency shelved, and each look he gave her put another play in that plan of his.

Couple weeks back, he called her into the office.

When she went inside, he was watching something under his desk. There was a flickering glow, noises—sexual noises, moaning. He looked up, a sheet of sweat on his brow. *Mr. Swallecki*, she said, *you called me?*

'Yes, yes I did,' he answered, licking his lips. 'It seems like I misplaced your paycheck. It's around here somewhere, was thinking maybe you could stick around, help me find it.'

Uhh, sure...

After about five minutes, she was growing uncomfortable. He would point to areas, tell her to check over there, and each area she had to bend over, present him what he wanted: a nice view. She caught him looking down her shirt, there was a noticeable hard mass between his crotch.

She left after that.

'Don't you want your paycheck?' he called after her.

Just tell me when you find it...

It was behind the front counter the next morning, sitting there for anybody to take it. Not a word was spoken about it again.

She felt relieved when she turned around and saw Swallecki marching back down the front end, his clipboard out in front of him, his hand working a pen over something on his charts. He walked past Dianne who gave him a scowl that he didn't notice. But Maxine saw it, and understood. *Maybe Swallecki gave her looks, too.*

"Hey, Max, was thinking after this, you and I could head to Cory's, grab a few brews, eat some good food, how's that sound?"

She turned, looking over to Stanley, he was sitting down, he had a dark blue ball between his legs, a smile on his face, one of those lopsided kind of grins that only men like him had fashioned over the years, those self assured looks. "No, I'll be busy, sorry. But, thank you." She looked away, focusing on her work.

Dredging up another wad of phlegm up his throat, he spit out a lump of snot onto the ball, the rag pushing around the offending slime. "Ah, come on, Max, every time I ask if you want to get a drink, you shoot me down, what's up with that?"

"I'm always busy," she said flatly, over her shoulder. "Besides, don't you have a girlfriend?"

He looked away from her, another smile pulling the corner of his lips up. "Nah, I'm not locked down, if that's what you mean."

Allen cut the motor to the buffer. Fixing the slack in his glasses, pushing them further up the bridge of his nose. "You have a girlfriend, Leanne or something, you were just talking about marrying her, weren't you?" Crouching beside the buffer on the lane near Maxine, dislodging something around the gears above the pad. "I overheard you talking about it with Hardy the other day."

Stanley gave him a dirty look. *Cock blocker.* "Nah,

I was talking to Hardy about my *brother*, he's marrying his girlfriend later this winter, sometime after Christmas."

Maxine turned back to her work, another spray of glass cleaner on the screen. She looked down to Allen who was working away in the next lane; rolled her eyes over Stanley's bullshit lies.

Allen stifled a laugh.

"Look, Stanley, I really need to focus on this," she said without turning around. "I don't want to be around this place all night, I have things to do."

"Oh… okay, okay, that's cool. Maybe this will give you time to think about my offer?"

She faced him a moment. "Uh… yeah, sure, Stanley, I'll be over here thinking about it. But do me a favor, let me focus on these screens in silence, I can't work and think all that well if people are talking to me."

Allen was rising from his crouch, scratching at something along his nose, a smile on his face.

Maxine gave him a wink.

"Oh, cool, I mean… yeah, cool, Max, that's cool. Just let me know, I'll be right here polishing these balls."

Allen laughed.

Stanley shot him a scowl. "What's so funny man?"

Allen dismissed the question, or rather didn't hear it as he started up the buffer again. A line of golden oil ahead of him, the soft pad of the buffer worked it over, leaving a shimmering lane of glass behind him. His feet spread out in the gutter was a bit of a chore, but he was used to it by then, having buffed the lanes several times in the past; finding a comfortable niche to work himself into.

Stanley sat back, the rag rolling over the ball, another wad of phlegm slugged into one of the finger holes before placing it back on the rack.

As he went to grab another ball, this one orange and scratched up a bit, a light bulb went off in his head. *Polishing these balls.* "Oh, shit, yeah, I get it."

Maxine looked back at him, saw him laughing to himself, turned back around and continued to spray and wipe.

The armored knight was tossing out an unending wall of knives that bit into the one eyed monster across from him. Jumping and dodging the whole time, avoiding the fireballs aimed at the brave warrior. A final three knives flew across the screen and blew apart the foul demon in a flash of pixels in a welcoming note of victory; the drop of a key allowing access to the next level.

"Yes, finally! I *finally* fucking did it!"

Jeremy turned around to tell Allen the good news, but all he saw was an impatient looking Swallecki, that clipboard banging against his thigh. His mustache twitching, those eyebrows squeezed together and his stomach lurching with each breath—like a breathing pumpkin.

"Mr, Swallecki, sir, I—"

"Save it, Jeremy. Now, I thought I wouldn't have

to be watching over *you*, but it looks like I'll have to keep a closer watch on you after all."

"No, I was finishing up on the cabinets, and the game just started playing by itself, so I was trying to find a way to shut it off." Jeremy gave his best shit eating grin.

Swallecki smirked. "Are you an asshole, Jeremy?"

"*Me?* No sir, um…why would I be an asshole?"

"Because your standing here blowing shit in my face!"

"I, uh…"

"Hurry up and clean those toilets, I smelled something foul in there when I was taking a piss."

Stanley's shit. Goddamnit, I forgot about that. "Yes, sir, I'll get right on it."

"That's what I like to hear."

Swallecki gave him a look before turning around and headed back down the strip; likely to his office to play with himself, Jeremy was thinking. He knew about the TV under the desk and what he watched on it in when he was alone, and sometimes not alone.

"Oh, and Jeremy?"

Jeremy stiffened, facing Swallecki who was near Dianne. "Yes, sir?"

"I don't have to worry about you playing with whatever is making that smell in there, do I?"

"God no—no sir!"

"Alright then," noticing a whole lot of eyes on him, he said, "Back to work people!"

With the music raging in the headphones cupped over his ears, his hair swinging, his head bouncing, Hardy leaned back, his hands miming an air guitar. The place around him was a shambles: rags balled up, hanging from work benches, knotted about. Tools were heaped in no particular order, used and greasy. Brand new bowling pins and balls sat neatly in tall metal racks, awaiting the day the crew put them to good use. Along the wall, to the right of the warehouse door, were the back ends of the pinsetter machines and ball returns, blue plastic crates were spread out near these, crammed with replacement parts; belts, bearings, bushings, ready to replace any faltering issues in the system. Near the far exit, leaning up against the shelving unit that held the microwave, a cream colored garbage receptacle was packed tight with old food wrappers and cartons. Above were a bank of florescent tubes missing the plastic coverings that were supposed to protect the fragile surface of the glass.

The door swung open to the warehouse.

There were feet padding over to him, but Hardy didn't notice—or hear much of anything, except for that trash metal stabbing down his ears with an atrocious set of notes. *Cannibal Child Eaters,* the band currently blowing a stream of scratching voices in his head. One of his favorite groups. Incidentally, one of Joanne's, too.

Hardy was screeching out another miming guitar solo when the man shadowed over him. A large hand came reaching out, the fingers squirming, slowly. Then with a sudden jolt, those fingers clamped around Hardy's shoulder, twisting him around.

Hardy coughed out a scream. "What the hell, Swallecki?" Pulling his headphones down around his neck. "You scared the living shit out of me!"

Face red, eyebrows again pulled tight, his face a mask of hate. "What the hell are you doing, boy?"

"I was just starting to clean, until you pulled that shit you just did."

"You going to give me excuses, too?"

"What excuses?"

Swallecki motioned with his pudgy digits for Hardy to roll down the volume on his cassette deck. "That's better. Don't know *how* you can listen to that junk."

"It's good shit, Swallecki, you should relax and listen to it sometime."

"Who can relax with that horrible music? It's like something you listen to before raping a farm animal, or butchering a classroom, what's wrong with you?"

Hardy laughed. "Damn, Swallecki, it's nothing like that, though the classroom," he ruffled the slight amount of growth on his chin, "I can see that as an album cover."

"Enough of this conversation, I didn't come in here to discuss your issues. I'm wondering why this place looks like a tornado blew through here?"

"Well, I haven't gotten around to cleaning it yet," Hardy said, dumbfounded.

"Well, why the *hell* not?" Swallecki shouted.

"Because you're in here talking to me."

"Look, Hardy, no more of that juvenile horseplay. We need to get this shit done, and by *we*, I mean *you!*"

With that, Swallecki uncreased his forehead, turned about face, and headed down the room, going for the door. He called back over his shoulder before leaving. "Keep that music to a minimum, it's hazardous to your health."

Placing the little orange foam covers back over his ears, his finger slipping over the volume dial. "How's that, Mr. Swallecki?"

Swallecki looked at him and smiled. "Because you can't hear what sneaks up behind you."

There was a door up ahead notched in the wall, a single light box bolted above. A few feet away sat a low brick structure, which surrounded a couple of heavy dumpsters that were packed with trash. The back wall of Silverside Lanes had been scrawled and defaced with a dizzying amount of graffiti. Weeds poked along the edge.

The cold wind that had been whipping across his face had picked up. A gauzy black screen webbed over the moon, dark clouds pushing in, the smell of ozone circulating. A storm was brewing; mixing up there somewhere, about to open up and drown this pathetic little town; stab at the land with bolts of blue lightning. He could see it now. A precursor; an ushering of his arrival of sorts.

The door was nudged open, a little bit at first, then it flew back, a foot kicking it out. A man came out of there, dragging an overburdened trashcan behind him. Black hair hung past his face, over his shoulders. Black shirt with a skull, black shorts.

Warner flattened himself against the wall, keeping close to the weeds and shrubs growing up around him.

The man was oblivious. His head was rocking up and down, Warner could hear the music ringing around the man even over the wind whistling somewhere out in that field just ahead of him.

There was nothing around him, nothing to pick up, use as a weapon. His fists balled up, his knuckles white. He would have to take this one apart the old fashioned way. With his hands.

"The fucking fat sonofabitch," Hardy said under his breath. "I hope he chokes on one of those little crumble cakes he's always eating." Grabbing the trash can with both hands, he upended the thing over the dumpster, smacking the bottom of it, dislodging anything stuck in the confines. A hollow echo resounded, confirming it had been emptied. He placed it upside down near the door. Took a seat on it.

He dropped a hand in the side pocket of his black cargoes.

A pack of Marlboro reds in his hand. Taking one,

he wedged it between his lips.

A silver zippo in is fist, he rolled the igniter across his leg, a flame flitted against the wind. The end lit, he pulled until the cherry sank down a bit.

Blowing a rolling plume from his lips, he looked out across the field, up towards the sky. "Looks like a storm is headed in."

Another long drag. More smoke pushing down his shirt, circling the skull in a misty haze.

He ran a thumb over the volume dial when one of his favorite tracks of *Corpse Fornicators* came shrieking over the waves. "Oh fuck yes! Love this one!"

Hardy leaped forward from the trash can, another one of those ridiculous miming rituals of his. Long black hair caught in the wind, his eyes sealed tight, locked in some world within, he never saw the shadow fall over him, but felt the air blow from his lungs as the fist sent him reeling back through the doorway.

Landing hard on his back, he raised his head, shaking out that funny feeling he had right then in his head. His chest was rising with effort, trying to regain some of that stolen air. His hands pressed on the cool cement flooring of the warehouse, he looked around himself in a daze, a thrumming pain in his gut. "What the *fuck!*"

His eyes blinking to focus, he saw something.

Right there in the frame of the door. A big man; a face cut up in scars, a mechanics suit or something resembling one covering his body. The light above the door outside tossed bold shades down over his features, bringing to life that hideous face of his; twisted into some sort of Halloween fright mask.

Hardy would scream if he was anybody else, but what he wanted more than anything right then was to spring that blade out sitting in his pocket, put some more scars over that face for what that ugly motherfucker did.

Righting himself, swaying a bit at the pain inside of him, one arm holding his gut, his other hand digging out the switchblade. A click, and the blade stabbed out, a glint of silver reflected back at Warner. "What the fuck man, what's your fucking problem?"

Warner took a step inside, the door slamming behind him, those eyes of his simmering and full; like two boiling black suns. He needed to kill this man, feel the blood pour into his hands, down his fingers, maybe paint his face with a few streaks. He moved forward.

"Take another step Jack in the Beanstalk, and I'll open up that fucking throat of yours."

But Warner dismissed the guy and his rambling.

Hardy jabbed out with a grunt, the blade nicking Warner in the gut, sinking just past the tip. He removed it, holding it out in front of him, the end dripping blood. "You like that big man? I got more of it—come on!"

Something went absolutely cold and dark inside of Warner. He didn't like being stabbed. The pain was minimal, but the *blood*—he could feel it oozing down his waist, feel its warmth, and Warner hated to feel his own blood on his skin. He took a giant step forward, closing the gap in a flash. His fist sprung out, the thick fingers found Hardy's face, clamping down with a pressure that was suffocating.

Hardy tried to say something, but whatever it was had been lost in the meat of Warner's palm. Instead, he continued to lash out with the knife, hoping to strike some meat, open up some gashes, anything to push that big lumbering sonofabitch away from him.

Warner was tired of the games, it was time to act.

He managed to grab hold of the arm swinging the knife. His strong fingers enclosing over Hardy's forearm like a steel cuff. With little effort, and a twist, Hardy's bone snapped, and he screamed, but whatever force was behind the pain was absorbed by Warner's thick palm.

The blade dropped to the ground.

Holding the struggling man in place, his arm swinging around by its new joint, Warner scooped up the knife.

Pushing the man away from him, Hardy landed on the table that was a good leaping distance away. He was squirming and screaming, shouting out things that Warner wasn't hearing. Warner's eyes were focused on the blade that looked tiny in his hand; the point bloody; the blade gleaming off the florescent lighting; he licked his dry lips.

Hardy was rolling around on his back over the table, clutching at his limp arm that looked more like rubber than flesh right then, like a worn out elastic band. He lifted his head, and screamed when he saw the big man barreling down on him. Hardy tried to roll away, but it was too late. Warner's hand squeezed the man's throat until a crack popped in his neck. The blade came down hard after that, punching a hole into one terrified bulging eye. The tip lanced the eye like a boil, blood jetted, spraying Warner across the face. The length sank to the hilt, tacking to the back of Hardy's skull like a ten penny nail.

Grunting, Warner twisted at the handle, cork-screwing the blade around, cutting, scraping, grinding away at the orbital bone.

Hardy's screams became a strangled whisper of broken airways. Each throaty moan whistled from his neck like a congested flute.

Warner jerked at the blade, but it wouldn't budge. Another jerk and Hardy's head came off the table with it, a pale juice was oozing around the knife handle, blood was spilling out of his mouth.

Letting go, Hardy's head smacked the table.

Warner looked around. He needed something to work with.

An awful grin slashed across his face when he saw it.

His boots smacked away, echoing deeper into the warehouse.

Hardy continued to moan that horrible throaty sound.

Warner was back, hovering over him, his shadow long and wide.

Blood bubbles were pushing from his mouth, more of that white creamy juice was leaking and running into his long black hair, mixing up with the oil that had stained it for so long. Hardy's one good eye was failing. He couldn't see much of anything, but he could still feel, and what he was feeling was a white hot agony burning in his brain. Images were flashing, mostly illustrations of gore and blood; album covers and posters he had pinned to the walls in his apartment. All those macabre bands screaming in his head, the covers alive and animated, crawling things, flaming eyed ghouls, hunched over pale cannibals, all reaching for him, then in a moment of clarity, Hardy saw it:

Warner had the bowling pin in one big hand. Swinging it down like a hammer, striking the stiff handle of the switchblade, causing it to slip deeper into the ocular pit. Another swing of the pin drove the handle completely inside, only a faint sliver of the handle was visible. Blood and brain slime pumped from the opening, flooding behind his head, slowly forming a wide sticky pool that dripped onto the stone floor.

The bowling pin at his side, a spray of blood dusted over the smooth white surface, his tongue rolled along his lips as he looked on his work. Blood was still filling out over the white of the table. He needed more of it; much more blood. But first, he had to find a way to lock this place down. He didn't want anybody to check out once the fun began. There had to be something around this place to secure the front door.

His eyes fell to a chain lying in a coil on a shelving unit.

Now he needed something to secure it.

Then something caught his eye: a ring of keys were hanging off Hardy's belt, a carabiner holding the set in place, like something a janitor would use. He jerked it loose, pulling a belt loop with it. Grabbing the chain that slid off the metal shelf like a dead snake, he pushed open the door and headed outside, into the rain that was starting to fall.

He was standing just outside the entrance, peering through that ugly looking mural that crossed over the door like prison bars, which would come in handy to prevent any superhero shit of jumping out the windows once the blood started to flow.

The storm was kicking up, grumbling underfoot. Wind was screaming over the black parking lot, the moon was all but smothered by darkening clouds boiling overhead. There was a lone vehicle puttering past on the road, oblivious of the terror lurking near the lanes.

Running the chain in and around the handles, securing them tight with the carabiner, giving it a few soft tugs, his lips curled in satisfaction. Even with the door locked from inside, the nest of chain was strong and tight.

Rain smacking his face, flicking against his clothes, he moved back to the warehouse.

Once inside, he needed to find something to secure this exit, too.

Racks of balls and pins sat neatly arranged on the tall metal shelving units, and coincidentally, they were only a few feet from the door.

It was taking a moment, but after a few, Warner managed to topple over two whole shelving units full of balls and pins that would bar any attempt at evasion. An impassable mountain of weight that would require the effort of a team to remove before Warner tore through them in an onslaught of hacking barbarity.

Now the real fun would begin, but first, Warner needed a weapon.

CHAPTER 6

Sheriff McCarthy took another bite of the heavy sprinkle, pink icing donut, crumbs falling from his mouth, rolling down his tan blouse. "What's this poor bastards name?"

One of the deputies, Merv Clyde, checked the wallet again. "Cray Carter."

McCarthy took another look at the man spread across the hood. His face was missing most of its skin, tiny slivers of glass bit into the skull beneath, jammed in his mouth, and there was that big curving slice of windshield stuck in the boys neck. And from the looks of it, that had been the main culprit of squeezing most of the blood from his body, which at the moment was being washed away by the increasing rainfall that was opening up overhead.

McCarthy snapped the umbrella above his hat. Shoving the last of the donut in his mouth, he walked over to the other man slumped against the Viero. Kicking the dead man's Italian Oxfords. "Who's pretty boy here?"

Deputy Clyde, trying to escape the rain by sticking close to the sheriff, moved forward, checking the man over for some ID. "I'm not seeing any-thing, sir."

"Check the car, dummy, look for registration, anything."

Clyde ducked inside the Viero, coming out a moment later with a handful of paper he pulled from the glove compartment. "It says here, Wade Dillon."

Looking down at the mess at his feet, sheriff McCarthy fished a smoke from his blouse pocket. A lighter followed. Taking a deep, long drag, blowing it towards the bloody mess below him. "Who did this to you, friend."

"Sheriff McCarthy!"

The sheriff looked up.

A young deputy by the name of Clark Stevens was running up to him, a sheaf of paperwork at-tached to a metal clipboard in his hand raised over him to protect from the rain.

"What you got there, son?"

"Found it inside the truck, sir. Apparently they were transporting that killer from the TV."

"What killer, son, give me names."

"Uh," Stevens flipped over the first page, his flashlight running over the soggy print. "Warner. Charles Warner, sir."

"The massacre fella?"

"Yes, sir."

"What in God's name were they doing coming into my district without notification?"

The two deputies in front of him looked uneasy,

not sure whether they should retort.

"Sheriff, over here!"

Another one?

A tall lanky deputy—Travis Miller—was waving the sheriff over with his flashlight.

Coming around the corner, smoke blowing from his lips, McCarthy looked at what had once been an identifiable man at one time, but now looked like something you flipped with a spatula.

"Good God, what happened to this one?"

Miller looked like he was thinking about it. His hands were moving around as if trying to piece together some difficult puzzle. "Looks to me sir, like somebody smashed his head in with something heavy."

Sheriff McCarthy rolled his eyes. "Good work, Miller." Addressing his deputies. "I need y'all to call up the right agencies and get on this now!" Taking another long drag, blowing it down his chest. "We have a maniac on the loose, and there is no telling which direction he took. I need patrols to scour this area, look for that sick bastard. And if you want ID on the suspect, I encourage you to grab a newspaper from any of these coin stands around here. I'm guessing you'll recognize him when you see him."

The deputies moved about, grabbing radios, switching channels, demanding assistance to the area. Already there was an ambulance rolling down the road, but McCarthy wondered why; what they needed was a hearse.

When he initially received the call by a frantic deputy Clyde, he figured it was just another Friday night accident involving a bunch of intoxicated reprobates causing hell on the town with a bottle corked in their mouths. He didn't think he'd roll up and see a bottle shoved into a man's face. Nor did he expect to find a man spread over a big hood, most of his blood swimming down the drain in the gutter; and the man whose head had been flattened by something powerful…

Nearing sixty years, a gunmetal mustache puffed over his thin lips, two dark eyes slotted in a face of ten grit sandpaper, barrel of a body shaped from an excessive diet of sweets and booze, and with over thirty years running around the town of Silverside, murders were a rare occurrence. He'd seen his share of shootings and stabbings, but mostly those were domestic affairs, involving family and alcohol, not random killings like these. Of course, he wasn't very familiar with lunatics running loose in his neighborhood either. Especially ones that had a body count higher than all the dead he had seen thus far in his life.

Silverside was a quiet little locale, nothing much to it. Mostly a blur to folks driving through. It had its good side and bad, like any other town tucked in the folds across the states, and right now, things were looking grim. *Warner, where you at, buddy?*

McCarthy was thinking hard when he pulled from the filter, watching his men run about like headless poultry, trying to impress him with their initiative and what not, but McCarthy would only be impressed when they found the sonofabitch responsible for these barbarous acts. And right now, that ugly man was somewhere out there, in the sheriff's stomping grounds, and to McCarthy, that was like kicking in the door to his own home.

Stubbing out the smoke beneath his boots, he pulled his collar tighter around his neck when a slip of cold wind blew over him. Looking out over his men being hit with the rain, working away at pulling tarps over the bodies, trying to preserve the scene in any way they could, he only felt one thing in his gut at that moment:

You came to the wrong neighborhood my friend.

CHAPTER 7

Working with Pauly had its up and downs. The man had little in the way for conversation, mostly just looking up at that TV, surfing for something to take his mind away from the pretty girl helping him out tonight. Joanne liked to talk, and working without talking was boring her, making her tired and focused on the one thing she hated: work.

"Pauly, you need me for anything else?"

Pauly looked away from the screen, the same glass he'd be cleaning out now for a good ten minutes in his hands. "Nah, I'll take it from here, why don't you go ahead and check on Dianne, see if she could use any help."

Joanne grabbed her coat from the table, punching her arms down the sleeves. "I think I will. Later, Pauly."

He got a good long look at her from behind as she pushed open the heavy door leading out to the lanes. *Get your mind out of the gutter, you're a married man, shouldn't be checking out other women, especially ones that could be your daughter.*

Turning his head up at the TV, there was more of that story about Charles Warner. The reporter was going on and on about the atrocity out at Venice Beach, all them young kids, butchered, hacked apart, pinned to walls with nautical equipment, it was a horror show.

Growing tired of watching it, he flipped through the channels, hoping to land something involving sports, or close to it.

So far, nothing good caught his eye. Just more and more about Warner, then something about the Soviets in Afghanistan, but he paid no mind.

Snapping the TV off, he checked beneath the bar, making sure all looked well.

Just beneath the register, concealed beneath the bar top, resting on two brass hooks, a double barrel 12 bore. Something he kept just in case any funny business ever headed his way. Though none had for as long as he worked the bar, there were times that came close. Like the instance when he had to throw out Wally and Hanson when the two of them got out of control, hitting those shots all night. The both of them ended up roughing up a poor young man and his new bride, telling the young newlyweds how they would give her a proper honeymoon, and by the looks of him, he wasn't fit for a woman of that caliber.

Pauly told them in his dry hard voice, to back the fuck off, and call it a night, or else things would get bad. Of course, being flooded in drink brought about a brazen attitude, changed who you were, and these two loved to switch things up when their eyes were glazed, and their blood was simmering at dangerous levels. Hanson brought out a buck knife from his boot, Wally had a little folder that snapped out and gleamed in the neon.

That's when Pauly pulled the long barrels out, thumbed the rabbit ears to the back and urged them to make a move. After that, both of the men ran out of their, screaming about some insane shit how Pauly was a certified loony to have a gun like that in a bowling alley. Of course he thought it perfectly sane, and just proved it had its uses.

Hanson and Wally still drop in from time to time, but no longer say much, unless it's between each other. Pauly still keeps a close eye on the men; you just never knew...

Straightening up the mugs, wiping down the counter for a second time, Pauly continued with his duties, hoping to all high hell that Swallecki approved so he could get his ass out of here before his wife had another one of those dreams.

Joanne ran another line of strawberry over her lips, smacking them to spread it around, she looked over to Dianne who had a beaten face.

"What's going on, Dianne, why you look so down tonight?"

"Swallecki..."

That's all she said, and Joanne figured as much. Keeping them all here, confined on mandatory bullshit, cleaning up the place so he would look good, hoping to still have a job after tomorrow. She knew plenty about the lanes opening up down the block, she also refrained from telling a soul that she had been offered a position there, so she could care less if the place closed up. She would feel bad for her friend though. She loved Maxine like a sister. They had been best friends their whole lives. Seeing her kicked out of her corner apartment, moving back in with her parents, would be a terrible thing indeed.

"Anything I could do to help put a smile on your face, Dianne?"

Rubbing the polish into the next pair of shoes, she broke out in a smile. "If you want, you can help me with these shoes. There's plenty more to get through."

Joanne peeked behind the counter, noticed a whole lot of shoes that seemed to still need attention. "Um, anything else? Like maybe I can clean up and around the counters?"

Dianne sighed. "I already did that, does it look bad?"

Joanne looked over the surfaces, saw the smudges near the edges facing any customer that would walk on up. "Uh, no, it looks fine, but it might be good if I do it over again, just to keep it shining."

Dianne smiled. "Thank you."

Joanne knew all about Dianne, didn't want to push any of her issues to light. She liked her, but felt she had to be easy around her, not say anything too graphic, or what not. It was a horrible thing that happened to her husband.

She took up a used rag that sat discarded on the counter. "Is this what you used for the tops?"

Dianne shook her head. "Yes, there's a spray bottle over there," she pointed.

"Thanks." Joanne grabbed the bottle, misted a few squirts along the long counter top. "Think Swallecki will keep us all night?"

Dianne looked up from the shoes in her hand. "I hope not, my daughter is stuck with my mom," she sighed.

"Ah, yeah, dude, that sucks. I had plans with Hardy, we were hoping to go back to his place and...never mind."

Dianne smiled, but didn't show it. "How are you two?"

"We're good. Just wish we had more time together, he's always working, and when he's not working, he's trying to get his band going on some gigs."

"Hardy's in a band?" Dianne asked, eyebrows raised.

"Yeah, they're really good. *The Death Dealers*."

Dianne looked up, a flat expression on her face. "What's that?"

"Oh, that's his band. They call themselves 'The Death Dealers'. They're scheduled to play over at Cory's next Friday, you should stop by. Might be good for you."

"I don't think it's my kind of crowd."

Squeezing a few more clouds over the counter, Joanne wiped away. "Still, it might be fun. Who knows, you might enjoy it."

Unlikely. "I don't know. Maybe. What time?"

Growing excited, Joanne said: "They play at 10:00, you'll love it!"

Dianne looked at Joanne like the kid she was inside; no responsibility, loose, living by the wind, she wished *she* could feel like that again. "It's a bit late…"

"Oh come on, please?"

"I'll think about it."

Dianne placed the pair of shoes back in the rack. Grabbing another, she started the sequence over again.

Joanne looked behind her.

Out there on the lanes she saw Maxine going over the scoreboards, wiping them down.

Stanley and Allen were out there, too, busy with their own tasks.

Allen had the buffer rolling down the lane, fighting at it as it looked to get loose from him every now and again.

She caught Stanley spitting in the finger holes again. *That's so gross, wonder if anybody ever pulls out a gob of slime on their fingers?*

"Hardy in the warehouse?" She asked.

Dianne looked up. "Yeah, Swallecki told him to clean it up, make it presentable."

"Ah…"

As if clairvoyant, she asked: "You thinking of going back there?"

"Was thinking about it," Joanne said with a grin.

"Be careful," Dianne told her. "Swallecki is walking around here, checking on things."

"Thanks for the heads up."

Joanne tossed the rag aside. "I won't be gone long, then I'll help you with the rest of those shoes."

Dianne smiled. "Thanks, I could use it..."

Joanne turned to leave, when Jeremy walked past her, one of those beaten looks on his face like Dianne had. "Why so gloomy, J?"

"Swallecki."

She laughed. "What's he having *you* do?"

"Cleaning the damn toilets."

"Ooohhh, tough luck."

She watched him walk away, his head sagging.

Joanne looked back at Dianne. "You sure you'll be okay over here, baby?"

"Yeah, go on, have some fun while you can."

She felt bad, but not enough to stay. "Thanks, Dianne, you're the best—I'll be right back!"

Dianne looked after Joanne as she hurried to the warehouse door, she muttered to herself, "Don't be too long."

The room had a musky, copper odor she couldn't place at first. She thought it must be all that oil Hardy uses on whatever gizmo or what not he's always working on.

Overhead, the lights were sputtering and firing off like there was a fuse acting up. She called out in a seductive, silky voice. "Hardy, baby? Where you at?"

There was only a flickering of light in response, throwing a ghastly radiance over the room.

Her jacket slipped from her arms, tossing it on a workbench to the side, she ran her thumbs beneath the straps of her top, rising the bands and letting the material snap back on her shoulders. "Hardy, I'm ready, baby, it's been too long, and speaking of something *long*..."

Just more of the strobing light sparking in flashes. "Baby, what's wrong with the lighting in here, you using your amps in here again? Shorting out the wiring?"

Growing uneasy, she stopped herself from removing her top. Moving slowly towards the back, her hands flared at her sides, there was something tugging at her stomach, like maybe she shouldn't be wandering around over there.

The smell was getting stronger. Reminded her of the time she walked in on her father field stripping a buck out in his shed. She remembers it with a clarity only the haunted could recall. Seven years old, big disc of a lolly pop swirling in colors in her little curled hand. Hair bowed and pristine, little frill purple dress, sandals. She could hear daddy in that shed of his, the one he said not to ever go near after his hunts. But like any child, curiosity pushed aside orders. There were sounds like metal smacking something wet inside. Peeking through a knot in the door, she saw her daddy in there, covered in blood that shined off his apron like wet oil, a big knife that curved like a terrible moon in his bloody fist. He was running the tip inside that poor limp deer on some strange contraption. Ripping off its thick coat, gutting the dead thing with a manic gleam. She saw the things eyes, black like barbecue coals, lifeless voids. She screamed and screamed, daddy went out after her, shouting her name, that long crescent knife in his fist, his apron gleaming red in the sunshine. She hid in a pack of shrubs, the smell was blowing off him, carried towards her on the wind; the odor of dead things; the hot-blood smell of things freshly killed.

That's what she was smelling right now. But that couldn't be, because there were no deers being slaughtered in here, only Hardy, and the smell of oil, and his gear, equipment, tools.

As if effecting the light herself, the closer she moved towards the back, the flickering became worse. She could hear the sounds of the storm outside gaining strength, hear rain smacking the roof. Then she saw it.

"Oh my God…"

There were bowling balls and pins scattered all over the ground, heaped in piles, two heavy shelving units leaning against the exit. *Why…*

Then she saw the body.

"Hardy!!" Her scream filled the room, bouncing back at her—hitting her with its agony. "Oh my, God, baby!!"

Her hands pressed over his chest, shaking him, screaming his name, hoping this was some trick;

that he was fucking around with her. But the only response was a whole pour of blood that oozed out of his eye, adding to the syrupy sticky blood coagulating on the table, hitting the ground in drops.

She looked at her hands, coated in sticky red.

She screamed.

There was a shadow rising near the exit, but it was hard to see just who, or what, it was. She hadn't much time to react as the shape of something white and thick came flipping end over end, smacking her in the face, blowing teeth from her mouth, scattering them over the warehouse like dice.

Joanne dropped, collapsed in pain. Blood was pouring from her mouth, her tongue was already swelling, thick and suffocating. Her lips split apart, divided, hanging loose. She was crying and moaning.

The shadow stood over her.

Her eyes traveled up to the man towering above. There were scars on his face, he looked familiar, but from where she couldn't remember. His eyes were black and dead looking as that deer so long ago.

He had something in his hand. It looked like—

The pry bar punched a clean hole into her neck, bulging her eyes from her sockets like a cod being pulled from the depths.

Her hands flew up, taking hold of the cold metal poking from her throat. She choked, blood spit out around the bar. She tried screaming, but only more blood shot out of the sides, squirting and spraying over Warner's frightful mask.

Warner lifted her as though weightless. Her feet off the ground, she was kicking out, struggling, wriggling. Warner was enjoying it. Holding her in the air by the handle. The flesh on her neck was having a damn hard time holding on to the weight, the bar started cutting upwards, tearing a line to her jaw. Blood blew out in a flare, spraying him in the face.

With his other hand, he spread it around, greased it over the bumps of his scars, slipped his fingers in his mouth, licked his lips.

Her eyes rolled over; her struggling eased up at the loss of blood that was pumping from her neck in hot red waves.

Removing the bar, Warner tossed Joanne over next to her boyfriend on the table.

She landed with a hard grunt that sprung more blood from her neck.

Throwing aside the bar, Warner lingered over her. Something of a grin opened his mouth.

Seeing this, tears ran down her face, mixing with the blood fast turning her skin into a waxy white like an old department store mannequin.

Warner plugged his fingers in her throat. She kicked and flailed at the intruding pain.

With a guttural grunt, his fingers dug around, poking at things, bypassing other things. Widening the hole like wet soil, his fist slipped inside. Hot blood swam around his fingers. Feeling her spine in there, he pulled at it a little, stroked it a few times, blood shot in his face. Using his other hand, he sank his fingers in beside the others. Feeling his way beneath the flesh of her neck, he probed further in until he felt the girl's spine. With both hands inside her throat now, fingers firmly taking hold of the slick greasy column, he gave it a tug, which caused a pop to come out of her neck, and more blood to spray out. Another harsh tug brought another crack and blood to ebb out. Growing impatient, he grunted and moaned as he pulled and twisted, blood shooting in his eyes. Now growling like an enraged beast, teeth gritting, his fingers fully embracing her spine, blood squirting and blowing from her throat, he put all his strength into his hands, and with that, he twisted and wrenched the lifeless head from her body, bringing an awful wet ripping sound with it. Joanne's chest deflated with a massive loss of air slipping from her lungs, a geyser of blood shot up from the gape in her headless corpse, splashing over the table.

Holding it in his hands, cradling it like that hat wearing adventurer ogling that relic in the *Raiders of the Lost Ark* movie, he examined it. Blood dripped from the neck, the eyes were white and filmed over in red, the tongue slowly slid past the split lips like a worm inching from grave soil.

Looking at the body on the table, he grinned, and it wasn't a simple grin, but a wide, lip peeling sort of grin that slicked up to the ears that cast him in an eerie ghostly flicker from the sputtering lights overhead.

Something caught his eye and he looked over and noticed along the walls were an intricate series of pinsetters, also beside each was a ball return. Near the end of the farthest one was a box, flips and switches all over it.

His grin grew wider now because Warner had a plan, and it involved a little bit of terror to start things off.

CHAPTER 8

He couldn't get over the girl on the screen. The way she moved over the man, her body undulant in its motions, as if a wave breaking and lathering over a jutting crag poking from the seabed. The long red hair swinging around as if caught in a draft.

Sweat beaded from his pores, leaking down his cheeks, dripping on his neck, soaking the collar of his shirt.

The movement in his hand below was working fast, pulling, tugging, flopping.

A knock on his door snapped him away from the screen.

"Who is it?" he cried out. "What do you want, dammit!?"

A muffled voice spoke through the door. "It's me —Pauly."

"What the hell you want?"

"I'm finished with the bar, was wondering if I can get out of here."

"Just a minute!" Pulling up his shorts, securing his belt, Swallecki stood. Grabbing at an old rag in his desk, he wiped it across his face, smoothing away any sweat beads. Settling in his squeaky blue felt chair, he leaned back, flipped a few pages over on the clipboard. "Come in."

Pauly entered, an expression forged from steel cut on his face. "Peter, I need to get the hell out of here. I talked to my wife just now, she needs me home—now."

Running his eyes over the paperwork in front of him, sweat dropping on the sheet below, Swallecki looked up as if disturbed from some important assignment. "It's *Mr. Swallecki*, Pauly, when you address me in any fashion, it's Mr. Swallecki, and—"

"Oh, don't give me that crap, Peter. You and I both know you're just trying to cover your ass, avoiding the chopping block that's sure to cut away the fat tomorrow."

Looking hurt, Swallecki sat forward. "I haven't the vaguest clue what you're speaking about."

"Drop the sideshow, Peter. I'm sick of this shit. Now, I'm finished with my share of the work, so if you don't want me breaking that TV under the desk, you better sign me off."

Swallecki looked insulted. His cheeks flushing red. "You can't speak to me like that, I'm your goddamn boss!"

"By *default*, Peter, you and I both know that shit. Don't act otherwise."

Swallecki's lips slit thin, pulling into his mouth, as if he were about to explode. "Listen here, and listen good, Pauly. You try and leave, and it's your ass —you hear me? I will cut your ass off the goddamn payroll, then how are you going to pay for those meds your wife relies on to curb those *issues* she deals with, hmm?"

The last time Pauly Jackson killed a man was too long ago, and right then, he was looking to kill again. How could this fat bowl of shit sit here and toss these words at him like ammunition? And this wasn't the only time, but over the course of several long months, Swallecki had it in for him; changing his schedule up at the last moment, switching his off days around. And to make matters worse, Pauly noticed a lack of hours registered on his paychecks. He brought the issue up to Swallecki many times, but he always feigned, acting ignorant of such things. *I'll look into it*, he would say. Of course, he never did. Pauly called up Mr. Henderson one evening after shift, explained to him what was going on, but all he managed to say in return was 'he'll get to it' which he never did, or if he had brought up the complaint with Swallecki, nothing ever came out of it.

Over the years they went from being somewhat comfortable with one another to outright enemies. It happened once Swallecki snatched that management position that Pauly was next in line for. His wife was going in for back surgery at the time, Pauly had to take a couple weeks off to handle things for her, watch out for her, and that's when Mr. Henderson, the big boss, went with the next name on his list. After that, a bitter animosity developed, which then turned to hatred and loathing. And over the years, especially the last few months in particular, Pauly's health was deteriorating, going dark, something inside his mind looking and reflecting back on all the hell he'd been through, and at work, he always kept a fifth in his pocket for when his nerves started firing off at the wrong time.

Pauly looked at Swallecki with a hate filled gleam in his eye. He was imagining slitting open that pile of grease, watching his insides blow from the gas bulging in his belly. Maybe take that shotgun of his, stomp in here, give him both barrels to the face, spread that smug look on him over the wall. It was a thought, and it was taking on a dark shape, showing him just how satisfying it might be.

"You know what, Swallecki? I've had it up to here with this high and mighty outlook you've been living with. Sitting there, in your little cheap throne, speaking to me with such disrespect. I'll tell you what, you keep up with that bullshit, I'm fixing to do something about it."

Swallecki laughed, padding more sweat from his brow. "Oh yeah, macho man? And how do you plan on going about that? I know how you spend your days. One bottle at a time, eh, Pauly?"

Pauly had a tick pulling at his eye right about then. Shaking his head. "You know what... I think I *will* stick around..."

"That's a good bee. Now go help the others who aren't finished just yet, that *was* the deal—remember?"

Pauly's face looked more stone than flesh. "Keep pulling on that little dick, *Peter*."

With that, Pauly stormed from the office, something going cold in his mind.

A door slammed somewhere in the building, echoing over the lanes. It came from the down the hall, past the restrooms, most probably Swallecki's office. Allen and Stanley expected to see a bumbling blob come pouring out of the corridor with a clipboard, but instead they only saw a pissed off looking Pauly, face red as a baboons ass.

Something about the way he stalked past the lanes, past Dianne, gave them both pause. The bar doors flew inside after Pauly gave them a good boot, the power nearly causing both doors to swing back in his face, but he caught them just in time with a thick forearm. Once he slipped inside, the doors still swinging until each side eventually sealed, Allen and Stanley looked at one another.

"Damn, Swallecki must have pissed him off," Allen stated.

"You think? I ain't never seen him so mad—you see his face?" Stanley asked.

"Yeah, boiling red." Locking the handle back on the buffer, Allen began to change the pad, feeling it was time for a new one. "What do you think happened in there?"

"Probably more of Swallecki's bullshit," Stanley told him, still polishing over those balls. "Or else

Pauly caught him beating off."

Finishing with the pad, Allen raised himself, cord in hand, aiming to plug it back in the wall. With a chuckle he said, "You really think that was it?"

"Knowing Swallecki, I'd say it's possible. He's one perverted weirdo. You see the way he's always looking at Maxine?"

Maxine was working over one of the last score screens on the lane, she turned at the mention of her name. "What's that?"

Stanley looked up from the ball in his lap. "Huh? Nothing, we were just talking about Swallecki."

She gave them both a crooked look and turned away, wiping and spraying.

Allen looked after her, making sure she couldn't hear, he lowered his voice. "What do mean *looking* at Maxine?"

"You never seen those looks he gives her?"

Either Allen never paid much attention, or rather could care less. He was only at the lanes to earn a paycheck for more comic books and videogames, not really up to making friends or getting involved in those little workplace theatrics.

"Nah, I never noticed."

Stanley laughed. "Yeah, his eyes swell up like donuts whenever she walks near him, trying his best to glimpse what's hidden under those clothes. Can't say I blame him, though." He looked over his shoulder, watching Maxine. Her ass was swinging as her arm worked over the monitor, the way her black ponytail bounced. "Look at her, she's fucking *sexy*."

Allen looked over. "Yeah, she's beautiful."

"*Beautiful?* Come on, Allen! She ain't your sweetheart, that girl is pure sex, look at those tits, that ass; her lips could do wonders, man."

"What do you mean…Oh…"

Stanley laughed. "There you go, use that brain for something other than reading those crappy comics of yours."

"My comics aren't crappy."

"ALL comics are shit, Allen."

Allen ignored him. Plugging in the buffer, he took the handles, unlatched the lock, had it humming over the lanes a second later.

Stanley spit another wad into the thumb hole of the latest ball before placing it back with the others. He stood up, brushed himself off, straightening his shirt. Running a hand through the thick wave of dark hair. "You got this," he said to himself.

Sauntering up, a big grin on his face, he pinched Maxine's calf.

She turned abruptly. "What the hell—what are you doing?"

"Take it easy," he said. "Didn't mean to startle you."

Maxine glared at him with those frosted green eyes. "What do you want?"

"Damn, Max, why you so cold?"

"I'm busy—just want to finish up here so I can get going."

"You really think Swallecki's going to just let you leave that easy?"

"What do you mean?" she asked, looking back at him.

"I mean, the cow will probably be keeping us all night into the early morning, knowing him."

"He can't do that."

"Afraid he can."

Maxine turned away, walking back down the step ladder. She folded it up and sat it back down in the next lane—the last one. "Not legally, he can't."

"Who's going to say anything?" he asked her with a laugh. "Everybody's afraid of losing the only job that's available to them right now. Nobody is going to snitch on Swallecki."

She looked away as she ascended the steps.

Stanley kept his eye on her, watching those long legs reach up. "I was hoping you thought about my offer?"

"What offer?" she said with annoyance.

"I asked you earlier if you'd like to grab a beer, get some food after were done here."

"Well, according to *you*, we'll be here all night— remember?"

"We can still get breakfast, or maybe tomorrow night I can take you for that dinner?"

"No, I don't think so," she stated flatly.

"Why the hell not?"

"Because I have plans."

"Tomorrow night?" he said incredulously.

"Yes—tomorrow, Sunday, and the whole rest of

next week."

"What did I ever do to you to get such an icy shoulder, Max?"

"Stanley," she said, descending the steps again, setting the cleaner and rag down. She got up close, addressing him like a child who had trouble understanding even the most rudimentary of explanations. "Listen...I'm not interested in you. *At all.*"

She smelled wonderful. A mix of so many different flavors that curled in his nose. A field of blooming spring flowers. He wanted to grab her, pull her close, works his hands over her. "Too manly for you, huh?"

She rolled her eyes. "You wouldn't understand."

"Try me, baby."

"I'm just not interested."

"What's the matter, you a carpet muncher?"

She focused on her work, not bothering to comment on his immaturity.

"Wait a minute," he said, rubbing at his chin. "It would make so much sense now—yeah, you're one of those dike girls, is that it?"

Maxine sprayed another spot, wiping it away.

"Holy shit!" He laughed, a bellowing laughter that ripped over the lanes. "Maxine is a dike!"

Her face sheeted over red. She knew how Stanley loved to talk, to spread rumors, circulate those rumors like a child on the playground. Even adding his own twist to such things. She could see it already, tomorrow, possibly even tonight; there would be a whole lot of eyes on her, whispers behind her back. But she didn't mind—not too much anyhow. Let them talk! She was proud, and done with being contained in the closet of her mind. For too long she had restricted her ways, but no longer. Growing tired of Stanley's push on her nearly every time she worked with him, annoying her with his brazen, masochistic ways. He just never got it in his thick, empty head. It was time to stab some reality into that coconut of his.

Lowering herself from the step ladder, she placed the cleaner and rag on one of the chairs near her. She turned, looked him in the face, wanted to slap that stupid funny look pulling his lips up; scratch her nails across those slit thin eyes. As it was, she grabbed his shirt with both fists, gave him a few tugs. "I'm GAY you moron, GAY, not a dike— okay? So no more, Stanley! Just leave me the hell *alone* for once. Between you and Swallecki, I'm *sick* of it!"

More laughter blew his nasty breath towards her. "You want Joanne, huh, that's it?"

His laughter was biting into her nerves.

Allen looked up, but couldn't hear much over the buffer, but whatever was going on between her and Stanley, he just shook his head, continued to run the pad over the lane.

Dianne looked up from the front counter. The same expression on her face she had all night, devoid of happiness, a bereaved looking mask. She saw Maxine out there, shaking Stanley who was laughing about something. *Crazy kids in love.*

Finally giving Stanley a good shove that landed his goofy guffawing ass in one of the plastic seats around the ball return, she grabbed the bottle and rag, started back up the steps, finishing up her work.

"I'm sorry, Max—sorry for laughing," he snickered. "It's just—damn, I never thought you were."

"Does it *matter?*"

"No, no, I, just...well, *look* at you! You were *designed* for a man!"

She turned around and tossed the spray bottle at him. The plastic container, sloshing half full, nailed him in the face with a thud.

Both hands went up, rubbing at the dull pain. "Ah, Goddamnit, Max, I'm sorry I said!"

She scowled at him. "Just get the hell out of here! Go bother somebody else!"

"Fucking bitch," he mumbled under his breath as he turned to walk away.

He staggered over near Allen.

Allen looked up at him, wondering why he was holding his face. "She shoot you down again?"

"Fuck you."

"Hey, what did I do?"

"Just, shut up, I need to get these done." He picked up another ball, one of another 60 or more to go.

Swallecki finished the video. It wasn't the first time he'd watched that one. *Alley Trash Whores #7.*

There was one girl in that video, a crimson haired vixen he just couldn't get enough of. He was thinking tomorrow he would try out the newest in the collection that sat packed in the bottom of his desk drawer.

Beach Bimbos in Heat.

A new one, he was told. He was looking forward to it.

Disposing of the soiled tissues balled on his desk, he fixed his shorts again. Thought about that run in with Pauly and started seething. *That old fuck is lucky I didn't fire him on the spot. Nobody speaks to Peter Swallecki in that manner! Nobody!*

Getting up, fixing himself. He made sure to cleanse the area of any evidence of what he had been doing in secret. *If anybody finds out what I do in here, I'll probably lose my job on some bullshit charge.*

Grabbing the clipboard, he moved out of the office, securing the door behind him.

The long carpet of orange looked neon under the razor tubing of lights running down the walls.

He leaned near the restroom. He could hear Jeremy inside, bitching and cursing about his latest assignment. *Good, good, Jeremy, you keep cleaning up that shit.*

Walking further down the hall, the area opened up with a pristine shine and glowing ambiance. Even from this distance he could see the lanes, and each one that Allen worked over with the oil looked brand new; sleek and mirror like, blazing pink beneath the glow of neon. The scoreboard monitors with their bubble screens looked fresh from the box, not a smudge or issue there. The counter top that enclosed the customer service desk needed a bit more work, but the walls around it had been neatly arranged, he was curious about the shoes and how they would look.

Moving further down the rough carpeting, he peeked through the spherical glass cutouts on the bar doors, glimpsing Pauly inside. He still had that grimace on his face, his cheeks still a shade red. *Keep it up, Pauly, and I'll can your old ass.*

Pushing past the bar, his eyes fell to the arcades. Jeremy did a fine job there. Each one looked fresh from the distributor. Even had that clean wood and chemical smell of new things.

Thinking about it, the whole place was smelling new. No longer musty and listing with age, the interior had a fresh odor, like one of those new car smells he keeps hearing about, at least that's what he assumed it would smell like.

Finally these people are useful for something other than bitching and moaning about things.

He walked the few steps down to the lanes, inspecting the balls racked in the interior of the dividing wall that separated the entry walk and the alley.

Taking hold of one, his fingers sank inside. *Looks good, but what…*

Pulling his hand away, a long thin band of slime hung from the hole and his thumb. "Stanley!"

Everybody turned at the sudden loud scratching coming out of Swallecki. Maxine was climbing down the step ladder, finished with her work, when she heard his voice booming around the lanes.

Allen nearly fell over.

Dianne looked on, bored like usual.

Stanley turned, the ball he'd been working over, rolling from his hands, hitting the ground with a loud echoing thwack.

"What in the goddamn hell is this shit!?"

Stanley's lips bulged, his mouth building with pressure, nearly laughing. "Uh...nothing, I mean, I dunno' Swallecki. Maybe gum or something."

"GUM?" He held his hand up, the end of his thumb drooling. "DOES THIS LOOK LIKE *GUM*, STANLEY!?"

His face continued to fill out. "Um," that was all he could take before the air in his cheeks deflated with a roaring laughter.

"You dumb sonofabitch, Stanley! I'm going to beat your ass!"

As Swallecki waddled and carried his weight forward like a raging bull, his face gleaming red, sweat running—something happened.

The pinsetters started dropping down the lanes, most of them empty, some full.

"What the hell is this, now?" Swallecki shouted, stopping himself over this strange happening.

Allen looked forward, unsure of why Hardy had started the pinsetters. He called over his shoulder.

"Maybe Hardy is testing them out."

"Why the hell would he be doing that?"

Now the ball returns were humming.

"That's it, I'm sick of this shit. I need everybody out front now—team meeting!"

A few balls started to burp from the returns, rolling around the looping metal trays. Then a loud grating, squealing noise started up, coming from one of the returns a few lanes down from them all.

"What's that?" Allen called over the noise.

"Sounds like something caught up in the belt." Stanley said.

"Which one?" Swallecki shouted.

"It's coming from over here," Maxine pointed. "Lane 9."

They all turned. Staring towards where the noise was coming from.

"Somebody get that shit working, now!"

Being the closest, Maxine started over. She ducked and peeked inside the hole that was black. There was nothing she could see.

The scratching, squealing sounds of mechanical gears was grinding louder. The pinsetters were dropping pins and sweeping them back.

"Goddamnit, Max, get your hand in there, fish it out."

She looked at him like he was mad. "I'm not putting my hand in there."

"I'll do it," Stanley said in a mocking valiant voice. "This sounds like a *man's* job after all."

Maxine wanted to kill him.

He strode over, an impish grin on his face. "Never fear, Max, I'm here."

She didn't bother with a retort. Just rolled her eyes, her arms folded over her chest.

Stanley reached inside, keeping careful not to get his fingers mixed up with the gears. There was something in there, like loose wiring maybe, but felt more like wet slips of filament.

"I'm not sure what the hell is in here."

He continued to spring his fingers around. "Wait...I think...Yeah, I got it."

His fingers clasped something warm and gooey. "Feels like an old rag got shredded in here."

"Hardy, that dumbass—probably dropped a rag and it got caught up in the gears. Did you get it loose yet?" Stanley shouted.

"Yeah, it's should be coming out n—"

His eyes widened a bit, not at what came out of there yet, but by all the blood that oiled his hands. He wiped it away on his shorts, some of it his red shirt, stepping back, coughing out a choke. "What —what the fuck is this?"

"What is it?" Swallecki shouted. "Stop acting like a baby."

"It's...It's...*blood*."

"Blood, are you retarded, Stanley. It's a goddamn machine!"

"No, I'm telling you—"

But he didn't need to explain, because right then a head came rolling out like a bowling ball after striking a set of pins. It was rolling around, patches of golden hair strung and wet with blood. Sections of the scalp had been carved away by the gears and belt, leaving a blood slicked peek of skull. The eyes were wide, violet, bulging and terrified, also very much dead.

Maxine screamed, a scream that shot through the place like an explosive canister filled with glass.

Allen moved closer to get a better look. "What's everybody looki—" He screamed—but it was more of a choking shriek that caused a spray of puke to slash over the bloodless face of Joanne that sat spinning in the polished metal tray.

Dianne came bounding up, leaning on the low wall to the lanes, getting a look at what everybody was shouting about. "What is going on?" Her eyes averted to the horror in the tray. She screamed, loud and piercing like Maxine.

Then they all screamed, including Swallecki who sounded more like a pig having its throat slit open.

There was a loud banging noise that they all turned to.

At the warehouse entry, a man was there, looking right at the five of them.

His features obscured by the lack of neon radiance that never found that corner of the lanes.

He started across the freshly polished woodwork.

Then all hell broke loose.

CHAPTER 9

He wished he would have worn gloves, or at least found a pair, because right about then, Jeremy's hands were covered in filth. Not dirt, or oil, but shit, piss, and toilet water. A few dots shot up from the toilet bowl with each thrust of the plunger, flicking him in the face. "SONOFABITCH! I'm going to KILL Stanley!"

The thickness of what lay coiled in the bottom had him gagging in his throat the instant he set foot in there. The smell lingered and it was hideous. He was imagining swamp green spores floating like ash in the air, clinging and spreading over the walls like fungal growths; a putrid, rank, nauseating stink of gaseous corpse pits bubbling in human refuse—yeah, it was that bad.

Thrusting down with the plunger, he again could not remove his eyes from the thing below. Like a snake slithering into the pipe only to die and leave its massive body looped and suffocating in a rancid pool of coppery water behind it.

Another powerful thrust pushed at the offending pasty goo that had trouble breaking down, instead spread around like hot tar, plugging the bowl with its consistency.

Jeremy tossed the plunger against the back wall where the rubber end bounced from the wall, coming right at his face like a shitty missile.

Luckily, his reflexes kicked in at the least second, and he ducked, avoiding the splatter that hit the mirror over the sink behind him. "SHIT!"

Now he had a new mess to clean.

This was becoming ridiculous. The whole time he worked with Silverside, never once did he have to clean a damn toilet. That was usually Allen's job, but of course tonight, Jeremy was relegated the assignment. *Well, at least after this all I have to do is vacuum the damn carpets then I can hopefully get the hell out of here, maybe make that movie after all.*

In the cart he had pulled from the utility closest just outside the restroom entries, he found a cone and a roll of yellow tape, black lettering ran down the length, saying *Out of Order.*

He pulled the door closed for the stall, dumping an orange street cone in front of it. Unscrolling a length of tape, he ran it up and down the doors in an 'X'. *This should work. Going to have to tell Swallecki that this toilet is broken. He'll have to get somebody in here, I'm not dealing with this...* shit, *anymore.*

Grabbing up a bottle of window cleaner, pulling a somewhat clean rag—the only dry one in this case—from below the cart, he burst a spray over the shit that spread over the mirror. His lips went tight as the rag brushed over the sticky mess. He had to fight the bile building back up his throat, it was like the first stab of the plunger all over again.

Then a scream, then lots of screams, all roiling and nearly blowing the door off its hinges.

"What the hell..."

He dropped the rag in the sink, placed the bottle on the cart.

Pushing the door open, the screaming was louder now, sounded like the whole crew exhausting their lungs at something too horrible to see.

Down the hall ahead of him, he could see them out there, huddled together.

This is strange...

He had a weird feeling pulling at him inside—some inherent feeling, something born from time immemorial, a universal characteristic all possessed on this world. Jeremy didn't know why they looked so terrified, but he had a feeling that he didn't want to see it.

His throat kept bobbing up and down as he swallowed with each step. He wanted to scream out, shout at them to stop what they were doing, but again, something inside him told him to be quiet, some innate trait passed through the genes was working away with his mind.

Jeremy kept close to the wall, his body lowered slightly as his legs bowed, a semi crouch as he crept along the wall, neon glow limning him in a pinkish purple haze. As he stayed low and slow, he neared the end of the hall, when, like everybody else, he saw it.

The man was huge, not really tall, just normal as a man could get in the average department, but when it came to width, he was a fucking monster. Big arms, thick as oak stumps, legs just as powerful and built. A squat head like a banged up paint can with corrugated stitching running along his face, dried over into pink bumpy scars that gave his face a frightening visage that could have been one of those cinematic works all the horror movies were using these days.

He was outfitted in something a mechanic would wear. It was sprayed in dark fluids, and most of the crew, trembling and huddled like cornered swine, thought only of blood, the blood of Joanne, and where was Hardy? Probably dead, too. Some of the red splashes gleamed in the lighting, other spots looked dried, but just as recent.

The crew were slowly looking for escape, but the terror of Joanne's head still rolled in their minds, and the man, a true horror, was moving slowly towards them, a look of absolute wickedness in his eyes. His black, dead looking eyes, that looked on them like a hungry shark after blood.

More screams and groans, moaning and whimpering, came from the beleaguered crew as the hulking man took his time moving to them, appearing to enjoy the terror veining through the crowd.

Dianne was fumbling for the phone beneath the register, but her fingers were shaking too bad. She had flashes in her mind, horrible mutated flashes, that showed her images of her dead husband, interspersed with this foul man moving towards them. A flicker of dread images that wove in and out of the man's crawling progress.

Swallecki was screaming, shaking; a wet warm spot soiled his crotch. He was shouting at the man, ordering him away, warding him back to whatever pit of nightmares he crawled from, slapping his clipboard in the air like swatting at a fly, but it did little to prevent the advance.

Allen was crying, his heavy cheeks soaked and wet with tears, glasses fogging over. He was moving slowly backwards, saying things under his breath, stuff like a scared little child would say about the ghoul in his closet. His heels smacked into the front counter behind him, he was at a loss of what to do, or where to go, waiting for the command of someone that had strength; the ability to whisk them away from this dangerous intruder. Allen continued his sobbing mercy as his head swiveled about, looking for escape—for salvation.

Stanley hopped behind the counter, grabbed a pair of shoes and launched them towards the man, but it did little. Then he grabbed another set, fast balling the brown and tan leather size 10s that smacked the man in the chest, and had the same effect as tossing pebbles at a mountain.

"Fuck this!" Stanley jumped over the counter, past Swallecki who was screaming after him. In fact, the whole crew was screaming at him, not just at the man anymore, but a combination of all.

"Come on!" he encouraged over his shoulder, hoping these idiots would have enough sense to get the hell out of there, make for the front door. But instead, the crew stood shivering near the customer desk; frozen, powerless to move, as though the man was hypnotizing them with his glare.

"Fuck it!" Stanley pushed at the door, but it wouldn't budge. *The lock you idiot!* He snapped the lock, then pushed again, but still the door held in place.

Grunting and mumbling under his breath, he pushed and pushed, until it started to give, then again it stopped.

"What the fuck is going on here!"

Everybody was shouting at him, higher than before, but he didn't care, he needed out of here, before that dude got hold of him, tore his head off and did something nasty with it.

He pushed and pushed. "Come on, damnit!"

Then he saw the issue. *A chain, there's a damn chain on the door.*

Stanley turned around as the screaming intensified, and when he did, Warner was standing right there, breathing on him like some foul beast.

Looking up, Stanley swung back and launched a fist into the man's face, but the effect, like the shoes, was useless, and now his hand hurt and was quickly swelling over like a cartoon glove.

Warner reached out, grabbing the man, and hurling him like an empty beer can over near the dividing wall where he slumped, dazed a bit from where his head cracked on the plaster.

More screaming and shouting blew over the lanes.

"Somebody do something!"

But all were stricken with a horrible paralytic terror that prevented reaction of any kind, other than to shout useless things and scream and scream.

In an utter flash, Warner closed the distance, grabbing Stanley by the neck, he hauled the man to his feet.

Stanley fought at this, kicking out and beating at Warner's arms, but it was like wrestling with the restricting power of a python. The man's fingers sank into his neck, all the while the evil looking man grumbled out something like a laugh, and Stanley's eyes bulged.

Warner pressed and sank his fingers with every amount of muscle that shot down his arms into his hands; surging, a powerful clamp that wouldn't release.

Stanley managed a toe kick into the big man's nut-sack, but again, it only caused a slight release from his neck, but Stanley used that slip and wormed away, dropping to the ground in a heap, holding his neck.

"Stanley, get the hell out of there, now!"

He started to crawl away, the man now facing the lanes, away from the crew, his hands obviously massaging away the pain that was just now webbing around his groin into his bowels.

"Hurry, Stanley!" It was Dianne, she was screaming and shrieking at him to get moving in a whiny, scratchy voice.

Warner turned around, his face twisted to that of a fiend risen from the grave. Like a demented horror, he shambled slowly toward the frenzied crew.

Pauly was truly at a loss as to what he was seeing. At first he was sure this was all some elaborate prank, most likely one of Stanley's doing, but then he watched as that big man held Stanley by the throat, choking him, and it was a bit comical, really. The way his eyes bulged and nearly popped from the sockets, reminded him of all those water logged corpses that he helped haul from the slimy mud craters impacted by air support in the Nam; also the ones who blew away like lawn debris once the concussive wave tossed them into the river of the Mekong. It was a brutal night battle that left many a good men dead and butchered into meat.

Now, staring out the portal from the bar door, seeing that lunatic out there, squeezing the air out of Stanley, slowly deflating him like a rubber balloon, he realized that this was a deadly serious situation, one he never thought he'd find himself in again. Also, the guy out there, he looked similar to that fella on the news. And wouldn't that be something? Charles Warner somehow ending up in a shithole of a town like Silverside, but how was that possible? Wasn't he supposed to be going up-state to that loony house?

Grabbing the 12 bore double barrel, he marched back over to the door.

Peering back out the window, he saw Stanley had somehow gotten loose, and was now crawling back over towards the others, dragging his feet like he had a problem standing.

Snapping the hammers back on the side by side, Pauly threw open the door, beckoning the besieged. "What the hell ya'll waiting on, get your asses over here—*fallout!*"

The commanding oration of Pauly's words snapped some sense into the waning, fleeting heads. Each of them looked over to Pauly, seeing him sticking outside the door, that big shotgun in his hands.

He raised it, the long barrels both pointed at that ugly monster out there.

"Inside, damnit, go!"

They ran forward, each moving quickly through the door, filing in like a unit of cherry ass recruits fresh off the bus in Ft. Benning.

Once inside, he looked back, saw everybody far inside by the bar, the low lighting tossing shadows over their petrified faces.

Looking back out towards the lanes, well, that big man up and disappeared like a magician, of course after a quick glance at his flank, he saw that man walking past the front counter, like maybe he seen something that he liked.

Pauly slammed the door, throwing the lock. "Everybody grab chairs, tables, whatever you can, toss them against this door, we need to keep that sonofabitch out of here, *move!*"

They moved as one, all manner of individuality molded away by the horror and dread of what awaited for them outside those doors. Even Swallecki, a man who *never* took an order, much less listen to the advice beneath him, readily moved like the rest, helping push shit up against the door, sweating profusely from his face.

Stanley was still gripping his throat, leaning up against the bar, his breathing had become hoarse and strange.

Dianne, Maxine and Allen, were each pulling chairs and pushing tables, doing what they could.

"Get some pool cues," Pauly ordered. "Slot them in the handles of the doors!"

Once the doors had been barred, everybody settled a bit. Pauly was keeping an eye out the portal windows, looking for that monster—or was it Warner?— wherever he went.

It was about that time that Swallecki came back around after dropping three shots of scotch down his throat, dismissing whatever sorcery had taken hold of him after Pauly tossed out orders like a drill sergeant.

"Why the hell didn't you shoot that asshole?"

Pauly just looked at him. The kind of look you give a child who just wouldn't shut his mouth or learn his lesson, no matter how much trouble he got in.

Nobody else was saying much. Dianne was biting at her nails, eyes round and wide, her red hair tossed about, frayed and sprung out like she'd seen a spirit rising from a grave.

Maxine looked distant, disturbed even, something in those eyes told a story that would take a lifetime to heal.

Allen was alone in the corner, still crying and mumbling things to himself.

Stanley was breathing a piping chorus like a flute clogged with mud.

"I asked you a question, Pauly, why'd you let that sonofabitch escape?"

"I don't know how he escaped."

"What the hell you mean? You let him walk right out of here!"

Looking distant, like he was thinking about things, Pauly kept his face out the window. "Somebody set him free."

"You losing it or something? Having a flashback on me?" Swallecki asked him.

"That man out there...saw his picture on the news earlier tonight. Something...Warner— Charles Warner. That man that killed all those folks down in Venice Beach."

"Ah, bullshit, Pauly. That ain't Warner, or whatever his name is. It's a goddamn lunatic, and we need to get the hell out of here! He's probably looking for something to help him get in here."

"Something has his attention, he went down

the hall," pressing his face harder against the portal, "I can't see him anymore."

"*Jeremy...*" Allen managed to choke out with a throaty reverberation. "Jeremy is out there, he was cleaning the bathrooms."

Slugging another shot, Swallecki slammed the glass down. "Now you've done it, Pauly—you essentially signed that kid's death certificate, letting that man get away!"

Pauly ran his tongue across his lips. "Remind me why we're even here this late."

Swallecki's face became red, swollen and blistering at the edges. "Don't go blaming this on me, Pauly!" He dropped another pour into the glass on the bar top, shaking the whole time, spilling most of what came out. "I wasn't the one who let that... *thing*...in here!"

Ignoring him, Pauly faced the window again, the shotgun resting in his arms folded across his chest.

"This isn't my fault, you hear?"

Still watching the lanes, Pauly kept his eyes keen.

"Joanne's death is not on me!"

Pauly looked back, "Joanne's dead?"

His question fell on muted ears.

"What about Hardy," Maxine broke in. "We haven't seen him yet."

"What about him?" Swallecki snapped.

"He could be dead, too."

"He isn't!"

"How do you know, Swallecki? I watched my friend go into the warehouse, and we all know Hardy was back there, but why hasn't he come out of there? You think he's hiding back in there somewhere? I *highly* doubt that. He's *dead*, I know he is!"

"Shut up, Goddamnit! Shut the hell up!" Swallecki grabbed the bottle by the neck and swung back, pitching it across the room where it exploded near the dart boards.

"Don't yell at her, Peter, because you're feeling a pang of guilt eating at that big belly of yours."

Swallecki was expanding and shrinking like a pissed off blowfish. "Don't start, Pauly, or I'll—"

"What? *Fire* me? You love your little pissant threats, don't you, Peter. As I recall throughout all the years I've been slaving this joint, you've threatened many folks during that time. Most of it pathetic, and let's not forget about your little pudgy eyes, the way they follow the good gals around here, eying them like your little fuck toys in those movies you like so much, and let's not forget about all those things you say about my wife, and how you scratch a few hours off my paycheck each week."

Swallecki was about to explode. The only thing missing was the steam blowing from his ears and down his nose.

"GODDAMNIT PAULY! YOU CAN'T TALK TO ME LIKE THAT!"

"Stop it! Both of you!" Maxine shouted. "We need to help Jeremy!"

Swallecki turned to her in a snap of rage. "We can't go out there, he'll kill us, you saw the front doors, that asshole locked it somehow! We're stuck here!"

"You can't just leave him out there by himself," Maxine said. Turning to Pauly, she pleaded. "Please help him, Pauly, please..."

"That boy is dead, Max—he's as good as *dead!*" Swallecki fumed, supporting himself against the bar.

Pauly spit out something lodged in his teeth, licking his lips again. "And so are you."

The barrels swung out, the trigger depressed, the shell exploded out in a wave of power. The cluster of metal pellets crashed into his face, the pressure collapsing the bones in his skull like shards of ceramic glass. And just like that, his head mushroomed out in a cloud of bloody brain gore, blowing back over the bottles behind him. Swallecki's body then slouched against the bar, blood shot out of his neck in thin erupting geysers, then he dropped to his chest, limbs flopping and floundering. Blood steadily oozed from the crater where his head had once been, smoothing out in a wide hot puddle, that glimmered pink under the lighting.

Everybody screamed.

Pauly reached inside his shirt, pulled out a fifth, took a pull, placed it back inside his shirt.

The screaming continued.

CHAPTER 10

The rain had picked up into a steady fall, tapping on the windshield like the urgent rap of knuckles. Blackened cloud cover overhead striated with blue forks in the distance, the rumble of thunder booming, it was a storm blown in from some far off sea port, at least that's how it felt.

Sheriff McCarthy was sitting in the passenger side of a patrol car, a pink box of donuts with the lid thrown open on the dashboard, trying to reach someone with the state police to help with the matter. But all he was getting was interference. *Goddamn storm, just won't let up.*

It sure didn't appear to be easing up any, at least for the foreseeable night.

On his way back to the station, dispatch broke in on the radio in spurts and chunks. What he could make out was that somebody had called and reported a body slumped in a gutter. Somewhere along 2nd Street.

The headlights hit it first, a man slouched on his back, his head sprung open like a bear trap, eyes glassy and swollen. His skin was leathery looking, shriveled and wrinkled by the downpour. He looked dessicated. Like something you would see washed up on a beach.

After a cursory sweep over the immediate area, sheriff McCarthy retired to his patrol car, figured it best to let the deputies mull and mutter over the scene while he tried the radio again. He was hungry, hadn't ate in a hour or so. Stopping by an AM/PM, he filled a box with donuts and planned on hitting the office for the remainder of the night, hoping to reach authorities that could help bolster a man hunt in his town, maybe get some answers as to why Charles Warner was passing through his town in the first place, and just why in the ever loving hell he was uninformed of such things; he also had a few choice words on standby for whatever excuse they could come up. But so far, that job had been relegated to dispatch. He told Maggy Cohen to go ahead and try for state and federal, but so far, like his own efforts, each attempt had been a failure.

Now worried the storm would build up enough to knock out phone lines and power to the area in due time, he had a new issue to contend with.

A fist pounded on the passenger window, causing him to startle. Through the sheet of rainwater washing down the glass, he could see the face of deputy Stevens outside, an umbrella bloomed over his head. Two small dark eyes thumbed in a thin skull, short blond hair hidden by a tan patrol cap, still a baby at the age of 29, he had a strange look of urgency to his face right then.

Cracking the window a notch. "What is it, Stevens, I'm trying like hell to get through to state." He sank his teeth into an overly glazed bearclaw.

"Sorry, sheriff, but I thought you'd want to know."

"About what?"

"Miller found two more bodies—in an alley back that way," Stevens jerked his thumb over his shoulder, indicating the location.

McCarthy nearly spit out the donut lodged in his jaw. "*More* bodies?"

"Yes, sir, sheriff."

Swallowing. "Show me."

He smelled it before seeing it, even over the storm, the smell of cooked meat and blood permeated, hanging in the air like a cloud of death.

At first, he wasn't understanding what he was looking at as he approached deputy Miller slightly bent over, holding his stomach.

It was the flashlight that cut into the rain that let him see, and it was a terrible sight indeed. *Some poor bastard, shoved head first into a barrel of flames, from the looks of it.* His skeleton was blackened, charred by the fire that had since evaporated, but his bones still smoldered and glowed like hot coals in a fire pit. It was a grisly sight, and deputies Stevens, and Clyde, both vacated their stomachs after finding a corner once catching a glimpse of it. McCarthy had to fight the boiling slop of donut stew in his bowels, working its way up his throat, lest he splash it all over that set of smoking bones in the barrel.

Then Miller pointed his light at the other body lying in a fast growing pool of rainwater. It was an awful thing to see, his head looked like it had been tenderized by a mallet. And not one of those little chef mallets either, but one of those big silly fun house mallets you use to whack at moles and clowns with. Like the man out on the street, this poor bastard looked drained, withered and water logged. His blood was mixed with the pool of water; a crimson puddle that was being constantly hammered by the storm.

"Goddamn, what kind of man does a thing like that to another man?"

This was all wrong. Sure he'd seen a few killings in his time, but nothing on a level like this. This... this was medieval. Some poor street man shoved into a flaming barrel, maybe even alive while burning away. Another one with a flattened head like the man they found earlier out near the wreck with the other two bodies. And the man on the curb...

McCarthy worked hard to prevent things like this from happening in Silverside. And so far, he would shake his own hand if he could, congratulating himself at a near impeccable record, but now the town had six dead bodies to add to the morgue, and maybe some more they had yet to come across. It was looking grim. With Warner on the loose, there's no telling where he could be, what he could be up to out there in the night. Even with the storm lashing over the town, he was certain it would do little to repulse Warner and his sick ways. No, the only shield standing in the way of Warner and his evil, was sheriff McCarthy and his loyal deputies. They just needed to find the sonofabitch.

McCarthy looked at the lot of his deputies ringed around him after coming back from his thoughts, umbrellas blossomed, each choking out whatever remained in their bellies, a seething anger went through him. "Alright men, gather around me!"

They moved slowly, holding their stomachs, faces glowing white with disgust. "Well, it looks like tonight we have a true madman on the loose. And what I need from each and everyone of you right now is commitment, more so than at any other time."

"What do you need, sir?" deputy Clyde asked him, his voice a bit cracked.

McCarthy looked at Clyde, saw those gleaming blue eyes of his glowing from beneath the hat, a blond mustache curled up over his lips. "First, I need these bodies pulled from here. Second, somebody try and reach Dan, ask if his morgue has room for three more. Next, I need you all to help rally Jefferson and O'Donnell, find where they're at, relay what I tell you."

He swung his light beam over the mess in the barrel. "If this man goes to evil lengths like these, nobody out here is safe. I want this man found, *hunted*, and don't go being soft on me either, we do this as a team. Once he's located, you call in support, don't go commando on me and take him solo, the man is dangerous, whether armed or not. And when we find him, make no mistake, I want him *dead.*"

The last word hung in the air like gun smoke.

"But sir, won't—"

"I don't want no buts about it! Once we find him, we *kill* him. Simple as that. A man that does something like this ain't no man, which in my book makes him an animal, a very dangerous animal that needs to be put down. The town of Silverside don't need no ruthless demon like this on her streets."

The three deputies looked at one another, a strip of lightning broke the sky, sending a flash of pulsing blue waves down the alley. Rain continued to pummel the thin fabric tarps of their umbrellas, three youngish faces wet and dead pan looking, the smell of alley trash, rot, and blood, went up their noses.

McCarthy's voice was powerful over the storm. "I know I'm asking you men allot, but you and I know that...that *monster* out there shouldn't be living! Goddamn state couldn't even administer the death penalty after what he had done to all them kids—and those little kids and their grandmother—it makes me boil inside! And now those doctors, they want to get him under the glass, study him, see what makes him tick, but that won't happen, not on my watch. I know ya'll are probably concerned about the fallout we may receive, but don't worry none, we'll do what we can to make it look legit, you following me?"

They all shook their heads.

"Good. Now get on it!"

The deputies spread out, bumping into one another after the command.

McCarthy rolled his eyes as they stumbled and ran down the alley, back to their patrol cars. His own feet waded and sloshed through the rain water, which only increased his anger. "Goddamn storm!"

Reaching his patrol car, he turned over the motor, switching on the heater. After a second the warmth started pushing out. He was thinking about Charles Warner, wondering why in the hell some knucklehead had to set him free like he did. And why was it that they were even parked in the first place, in *his* neighborhood.

Of all the goddamn places!

McCarthy thought he may have acted irrationally with his decision, faced with those bodies out there in the cold night; maybe a bit hasty in his orders. Sometimes thoughts occurred to a man in the heat of things, only to be regretted later after he's had time to think of his actions, but... this wasn't one of those times, and McCarthy knew he was providing a service to the state, to the country; wiping this menace from the earth.

Now he just needed his men to find this sonofabitch, put him down with a vengeance, but in the back of his mind, he was hoping to be the one who actually got to squeeze the trigger on this loon.

His car pulled from the curb, leaving his men behind, as he started his search, the rain pelting the hood of his cruiser, lightning flicking and striking with a silence.

And just a pistol shot away, the crew of Silverside Lanes was quickly falling apart.

CHAPTER 11

Jeremy was running faster than he had in his life. His heart kicked at his chest, his breathing was getting thin and stressed, not being much of an athlete, more accustomed to being another bump on the couch, a controller in his hands, pushing through a punishing level of whatever game had him intrigued at the moment.

He was down the hall, going for Swallecki's office, but the knob was stiff, locked and tight.

"SHIT!"

Turning around, he saw that man starting down the hall, waves of pink neon cut around him, his fists balled and ready for death. That face of his... it was similar to something he had seen in a movie at one time, *The Burning*, a grotesque mask of scars that looked more like pink dead worms bunched together.

Behind him, the hall ended with a utility closest shuttered with a black door, not a real good place to seek refuge, of course that only left him with the restrooms only a few feet away. He decided on the latter, bounding forward, throwing open the men's room, clicking the bolt secure.

Once inside, he looked around the blinding white tiled room. The nauseous wave of human gas still hung in the air as his eyes fell to the cart that sat near the three stalls. Attached around the cart was a mop, a broom, a spare plunger, a scattering of cleaners and toilet brushes, but nothing that would do any real damage to that walking refrigerator out there.

He decided on the broom, since its wood was thick and stronger than the mop. Holding it at an angle, he slammed his foot down on the end, breaking off the bristle head.

Holding it front of him, double handed like a spear, his mouth hung slack, eyes bulging, scared and wide. He swallowed when the pounding on the door started.

Easing back a few steps, thinking that man would blow down the door like that slavering wolf hungry for pig meat, he kept his hands tight— tight as they would get that is—because reality was: he was shaking, and shaking real bad. Even with the broom handle and its chiseled sharp tip out ahead of him, the fear was too much—especially one not accustomed to fending off the specter of death looming in on him.

He felt a warm trickle slide down his leg and soak into his sock.

The door continued to bang and shake, Jeremy nearly screamed each time, worrying that the door would soon come right off those little hinges.

Then as merciless as that pounding was, it

stopped—dead.

Jeremy didn't move. His breathing was still thin and ragged. The sound of his heart beating nearly drowned away any other sound there could have been.

Standing there, for what seemed like minutes, but could have been no longer than a few seconds, he slowly made for the door.

Leaning against it, he pressed his ear to the rough surface, listening...listening.

Then, a sound; the unmistakable clumping of footsteps coming closer to the door.

"Shit..." Jeremy backed away, keeping the spear out in front of him.

BAM

The door bucked.

BAM

It was shaking in its frame.

BAM

The handle, it looked—

BAM

Then the handle broke off, dropping and clattering to the ground.

Jeremy jumped back into a stall, shutting the door behind him, snapping the lock secure. He knew the futility of what he was doing, but he had no other choice right then. Hid body wasn't up to the confrontation of seeing that man out there, looking into those black eyes, that synthetic looking face.

The squealing of the door opening locked his

body up. Rigid, sweating, eyes shaking, body full of tremors, he slowly pulled himself up onto the toilet, keeping low to avoid poking up, exposing himself.

Boots started smacking into the room.

Jeremy could hear the man breathing, was wondering if his own heart was beating too loudly.

BAM!

The door to the shit stall blew open.

Jeremy swallowed.

BAM!

The walls shuddered as the stall door next to his smacked inward.

Jeremy felt like he were about to explode right then.

The boots stood outside his stall now, the toes visible. He knew the man was certain Jeremy was behind door number three, and right at that moment, the door shot inside, Jeremy screamed as he thrust out the spear like a legionnaire and plunged the spiked end into Warner's shoulder.

Warner grunted, dropping the bowling pin he used to batter his way inside the restroom, staggering back, taking the broom handle with him, blood rolled down his arm, dotting the tiles below.

Jeremy sunk back against the wall, watching the man grab and pull out the stock of wood.

Something inside of Jeremy was telling him to run, get the hell out of there, this is your only chance, and right then he did just that, shooting forward, turning left and bolting for the door.

Only Warner anticipated such a maneuverer, so instead of Jeremy running freely, away from this nightmare man, Warner knocked him aside where he went crashing into the bank of urinals past the stalls.

Shaking his head, he quickly recovered, starting for the door, Warner came forward, knocking over the janitor cart. A bottle of toilet cleaner came rolling over, it caught Jeremy's eyes. Reaching, he grabbed out for it, taking hold of the plastic neck, then Warner was on him.

His fingers were thick and tough, full of strength, and right then those digits were grappling around Jeremy's neck, lifting him straight off the ground like a noose, holding him against the wall.

Warner got in real close, breathing and grunting in his face.

Jeremy was kicking around, still holding on to the bottle.

Black dots bounced and jumped in his vision as his air quickly cut away, then in a last second attempt, he brought the spray bottle up, squeezed a mist of bleach into Warner's eyes.

Warner let go, Jeremy collapsed, holding at his neck.

Warner was falling back, clawing at his eyes, moaning and grunting like a primal savage.

Jeremy used this time to get the hell out of there.

Getting to his feet, he ran from the restroom, falling against the wall, the pain pulsing around his neck was making it hard to breathe. He continued down the hall, the lanes opened up to his right in a neon blur, to the left the front counter, and beyond that the bar doors and arcades lined against the wall.

He needed to reach the front door before it was too late.

After Pauly blew open Swallecki's head, the crew lost their minds, running around, finding shelter, either behind the bar, or under a pool table, even though essentially they were trapped, contained in this bar of blood, there wasn't much of a choice, unless they stood by and maybe Pauly decided he liked the result and wanted to pump another shell of buckshot into somebody else.

As they scattered like a group of terrified fowl, Pauly took another slug of the fifth, capping it and placing it back in his shirt pocket. "It's okay, it's okay, people, I'm not going to hurt you, I can assure you of that." Moving forward, the shotgun held low as though stalking game. "I...I only wanted to get Swallecki, the man deserved what he got! You know it, just as I know it."

The crew was trembling.

Allen was a sheet of tears, his face glimmering, glasses fogged over, his portly body was quivering, hiding beneath the pool table. He saw Pauly walking around real slow, saying things.

"I promise I won't hurt any of you, I like you all, but Swallecki, that pig deserved to die, he was a terrible man, a womanizer, a pervert, you don't know him like I knew him, and those things he did... always getting away with shit!"

Dianne held her knees to her chest, making herself as small as possible behind the love tester past the pool tables. She wanted to peak forward, see where Pauly was right then. The way he was speaking, she knew he had lost it, like something in had been festering in his mind just waiting to snap and right then, she was certain it had.

"Now come on out, I promise you all that nothing bad will happen to you, you have my word on that." He swung the barrel around, his eyes red, inflamed as burning meteors breaking orbit. "Come on, please come out of your little holes— drinks on the house people!"

Maxine was behind the bar, Stanley, too, was sitting back there, grabbing what he could to use as a weapon. There was a knife; a little carving knife Pauly used to cut lime and lemons with, not real big, but was sharp as a fillet blade. Maxine found a wrench and a pair of pliers, not much, but it was better than a bottle, which if used the wrong way would only break in her hands, cutting her all to hell.

"Stanley, why don't you come out here, we can chat about things, discuss where we go from here." The barrel knocked on the bar top. "No? You afraid to come on out from behind there. I know you're there Stanley, come on, come on, it—"

"HELP!"

Pauly turned at the banging on the bar door.

Jeremy's face filled out the portal. "Help me, Pauly, please, help me—he's coming right now!"

Pauly lowered the shotgun, a big wide grin pulled his rough cheeks up. "Looks like Jeremy needs our help." Rising the barrel. "Maybe we should lend him a hand."

As he started forward, Stanley sprung up like a jester in a wind up toy box, stabbing out with the knife, sinking the blade in Pauly's back which shot a bolt of white pain up his spine.

Screaming, he turned and depressed the trigger, blowing a hole in the into the wall directly behind Stanley. Bottles exploded, tossing out shards of glass and clouds of liquor into the sky.

"Holy shit!" Jeremy saw this and ran.

After watching Stanley reach out from behind the bar and stab a blade into Pauly, Jeremy screamed, more of a confused scream mixed with the horror of the situation he now found himself in.

What came next was a shotgun blast that tore a crater the size of a basketball into the bar behind Stanley, and that, too put some more confusion into the situation. *Why did Pauly have a shotgun, and why did he try and kill Stanley?*

He figured it best not to even try getting inside the bar. Instead, he made a run for it, but right before he did so, he saw that man was moving quickly, coming closer to him.

Jeremy yelped like a screeching cat, made a dash for the doors.

Reaching them, he pulled at the handles, shaking them hell out of them, but it did little. "Come on, what the fuck! Let me out, LET ME OUT!!"

Right about then something flew right past Jeremy, smacking the glass where it shattered like a frozen waterfall in a thousand slivers. A blowing gust of cold wind blew through the alley and a misting of rain. Thunder moaned and lightning struck outside. Jeremy cried out after seeing the bowling ball rolling away. Then he looked up and saw that man again, and he had a new bowling ball in his hands. A heavy looking red one.

Jeremy got to his feet just as the ball was tossed like it had been made of plastic. It came flashing forward, and before Jeremy could react, the ball punched into his chest, dropping him in a wide jagged pile of glass shards and rain drops.

His chest felt broken and battered, like a sledge hammer worked him over.

Flipping himself over, he tried to crawl, but there was a pain running along his torso that froze his arms up, and each time he reached out was like a knife blade cutting into his arm pits.

Warner was on him, he picked up the ball with both hands. Raising it above his head, he brought it down on Jeremy's spine. There was a resounding crack like snapped hickory as the ball impacted.

Jeremy screamed out as his body went rigid as a plank. Blood shot out of his mouth.

Warner raised the ball again, and brought it down like he was dunking a basket. The ball smacked the lower backside of Jeremy's head, and though that blow should have killed him right then—ended his pain—it didn't have that effect, but something inside his mind came loose, like a lobotomy, he was drooling blood, his eyes rolling around in puffy sockets.

Warner reached down and picked Jeremy up, which was like grabbing at a body that had been freezing beneath an avalanche, his limbs were stiff and solid.

Warner dragged him face first through the glass, then reaching the arcades, he raised up the young man, looked him in the eyes. Those eyes were rolling around like something you would see behind a mask, as if his own face was incapable of movement, Warner smiled at this.

Then with an aberrant thrust, Warner pushed Jeremy's head into the Ghost & Goblins screen. At first it cracked, fissuring the screen like a web, then another attempt broke it some more. Finally, a third assault on the machine blew the screen inside the cabinet. Sparks and smoke snapped and streamed out. But Warner wasn't finished.

Pulling his head out, he looked at the boy a final time. His face was a pulpy mass of shredded tissues and flayed skin flaps. Blood covered his face, sopped up in his hair like a sponge, the whites of his eyes were rolling, a gurgling moan pushed more blood from his mouth that foamed over his lips and down his neck.

Taking a fist full of the kid's hair, he shoved Jeremy's head back towards the jagged lip of the screen which looked more like the teeth of some nightmare saw. And with that, Warner ran the kid's neck across the ridge of spikes, back and forth, back and forth. The glass did fast work, ripping inside Jeremy's neck with a wet leathery ripping sound. Blood gushed out, running down the console joysticks. Sparks continued to snap and burst from the machine like bottle rockets.

Warner started to grunt, his arms were growing tired of the motions. Finished, he grabbed the head and twisted, jerked and pulled until it tore free, causing a jet of blood to splash over the arcade marquee. Jeremy's body dropped, no life to fire off nerves, just lying stiff and inert, blood pumping and pooling.

Warner looked at the face, held it close to his own.

He smiled at the way Jeremy's eyes slowly rolled up into his mind. He was wondering what Jeremy could be thinking in death.

Looking towards the lanes, an idea hit him.

Descending the few steps, he stood out on the lanes, a rack of pins lay ready and gleaming on lane 3. Reaching back, he bowled the head down the lane where it slid in the gutter.

Unhappy with the result, he stalked down the lane, grabbing the head, reeling it back, and pitching it forward. Jeremy's severed head spun around in the air, smacking headfirst into the group of pins where it blew them apart in a perfect strike.

Pleased with this, Warner had more blood to get his hands in.

And just as he turned his attention to the bar, the place went black.

CHAPTER 12

Pauly thrashed around, still keeping his grip on the shotgun, his other hand reaching back, tugging on the knife handle lodged in his scapula, which only drove the blade deeper into his muscles as he tore at it madly. He screamed out in a rage as he pulled it free with a squirt of blood, tossing it onto the pool table nearest him.

Stanley was fearful. Reaching for something, anything that would shake Pauly up, disable him, throw him off a bit so he could get away.

Grabbing a bottle, he threw it over to Pauly, but the throw was wide and hasty, so he easily stepped aside where it broke apart on the ground.

Raising the shotgun, he grinned wide as he squeezed the trigger, the rabbit ear slamming on an empty changer. He looked down —forgetting he had already blown off the only two shots the gun held.

His eyes fell down to the shotgun; he broke open the breach, ejecting the spent cartridges.

Pauly's lips curled up into a malicious sneer as he fished out two more shells from his pocket, feeding them into the barrels. Snapping it shut, he raised the gun, Stanley dropped just as a bellowing crack rolled out the end, blowing a thick chunk of bar top off in a cloud of splinters, the pellets crashing into a three level stack of bottles that exploded in a plume of glass smoke.

"Goddamnit, Stanley, I need you to stand still! It doesn't work unless the buckshot *hits* you, didn't you know that?" Breaking the breach open again, he pulled out the empty, tossing it on the ground, and replaced it. He padded at his pocket, a couple more shots remained.

"Pauly, what the *fuck* is wrong with you!" Stanley shouted from behind the bar in a hoarse strain.

"Ain't nothing wrong with *me* pencil dick, I just don't like the way you speak down to me, boy, treating me with such disrespect; like your pal Swallecki over there. All those things you say behind my back; about my wife, don't think I ain't ever hear what you what say when these old ears are out of range—I should shove this shotgun up your ass boy, give you both barrels, blow your ass apart!" Pauly laughed. But it was more of a maniacal tittering then something you would hear after a joke. "Now come on, Stanley, raise your skinny ass up. You can make it quick, or else I'm coming for you, and I can promise, if you make me come for you, I'll make sure you wish you hadn't."

As Pauly started slowly for the bar, barrels stretched out, the lights suddenly snapped and popped out.

A wall of shadows descended over the room

with the squeals of screams and shrieks from the frightened.

"Well, well, well, would you look at that. Now we get to play 'who's afraid of the dark.' And the winner gets a barrel!" Moving cautiously in the dark, he swung the shotgun out around him, thinking someone was near him. "Come on now, I hear you out there...*yes,* you're all moving around like rats, skittering about, scratching at the walls, looking for a hole. You think old Pauly can't see you, but believe me, my eyes work well in the dark, and it's only a matter of time before my gun finds you, too."

Pauly's voice was madness, sheer delirium. A shambling thing wrung of humanity, replaced with a crazed lunacy. *How,* or *why* he suddenly snapped was anyones guess, but right then, it mattered little to Dianne, who wanted nothing more than to get out of there, alive, back to her daughter, away from Pauly, away from that lunatic roaming the lanes. She sat forward a little bit, thinking he was near. He stopped speaking, but she could hear him out there, slithering around like a snake in its den. She was sure Allen, Maxine, and Stanley could hear him, too. The darkness held thick, bold shadows drew over the room like a dark sea. She thought of being in a casket, packed beneath six feet of wormy soil. Since her eyes could no longer show her things, she had to rely on her mind, her senses, and right then, they were playing with her, taking shape with her imagination.

She could hear things to a greater degree than before, like the blind. Pauly was moving slowly, she could hear him breathing.

"*Where are you,*" he whispered.

Dianne threw a hand over her mouth right them, stifling a scream that boiled up her throat. He was standing right there, she could see little of him, but he was *there*, only a few feet away, maybe closer, and he was breathing real deep through his nose; the sound reminded of her a gale blowing over a reed field.

There was movement somewhere near the bar, like something fell over. "Ah, so you're still by the bar, huh?" Pauly started over, doing his utmost to keep his movements muffled and vigilant, lest he trip over something. "I know this place better than my own home, folks. So come on out—let me get a feel for you." A few steps closer now. "You can help me place the barrel on your head, make it quick and clean, well, not so much *clean,* but quick."

"FUCK YOU, PAULY!" A flashlight popped on, cutting a path through the dark, catching him in the eyes.

"SHIT!" Pauly threw a hand over his eyes, his finger applying pressure to the trigger in reaction, but the action wasn't fast enough. Maxine struck out like a cobra, and swung out the wrench, striking Pauly in the temple were he dropped like an up-rooted tree during a storm.

"Hit him again!" Stanley demanded, jumping over the bar top.

The cone of light swung over Pauly's body, he was rolling around, holding his head, blood ran down the side of his face, the shotgun loose in his grip. "You little cunt! I'll rip your heart out!"

She swung again, harder this time, the blow tore some teeth out of his mouth, tossing them into the dark. Blood and spit gushed out. He tried to say something else, but more blood just slipped out instead.

"AGAIN!" Stanley screamed in near mania.

"*NO!* Damnit—we need to get out of here!" Maxine went for the shotgun, but Stanley was too quick. He swept it off the floor, bringing it to his shoulder. He was swinging it around, eyes wild and crazed.

"*Easy*, Stanley," she said to him. "Take it easy."

"EASY?!" he pressed it hard into Pauly's bleeding head. "You think he was going to go *easy* on us!?"

"He's done! Look at him," Maxine said, pointing below.

Stanley swung the blade of light over Pauly, holding it tight beneath the barrel. He was bleeding and moaning in his throat.

"Now give me the gun, Stanley, together we can all get out of here—alive! We don't need to resort to this, not like him, and not like that guy still out there." With all the insanity kicking off in the bar, it was hard to remember that just outside those doors was the *real* threat. The one with those black eyes and grisly face.

"NO!" I'm not going anywhere until help gets

here, that guy is a fucking psycho out there, and... and—"

"*Nobody* knows we're stuck here, Stanley, we need to get out now, while we can," she pointed at the gun in his hands, "While we have the power to do so."

She was as scared as he was, but deep down, she was pulling at energy she never knew she had, trying her damnedest to convince Stanley to keep it together, to see things with a clear head. But she also understood the circumstances. Pauly had lost it, killed Swallecki, and now it looked like they had made his hit list, too. And right now Pauly was laid out, bleeding from the skull, not much of a threat to anyone. Way he was looking, he would bleed out, die right in his own bar next to Swallecki.

"I'm not giving this gun to anyone! I'm not doing it!" With the flashlight held firmly under the barrels, he swung the beam around. Dianne, and Allen emerged from their holes, closing in on him, not so much as conspiring with Maxine, but they way he saw things, that's *exactly* what it looked like. "Look, nobody try anything," he said in a high screeching voice. "I'm *not* fucking around, I *will* defend myself!"

"Nobody is trying to hurt you," Dianne said in a shaky timbre, standing rigid and terrified, afraid of moving just a little, thinking Stanley would see that as an attempt at grabbing him.

"She's right," Maxine said from his left. "We all just want to go home, but we have that maniac out there, and he wants to hurt us—stop us from leaving here."

It happened in a flash.

Pauly's arms shot out, sweeping Stanley off his feet. He cried out as the shotgun fell from his hands, the flashlight, too, dropping and spinning a glowing cone over the room. Maxine, Dianne, Stanley, and Pauly, each went to grab it. Allen was grounded beneath the pool table, unable to convince himself to move. He just lay there motionless, breathing deeply, a hand over his chest, his eyes wide and worried behind the glasses, watching all this unfold in front of him—paralyzed by all terror of the night.

Pauly was pulling himself forward, his eyes gleaming in the light.

Stanley, on his back after the fall, turned over and tried to get to his feet. Dianne, moving slowly, thinking about hiding again, made little effort to recover the gun. Maxine was nearly on it when Pauly scooped it up.

Everybody scattered, except Stanley who dropped on top of him, fighting and grappling over the shotgun.

Stanley screamed out in his face. "GIVE ME THAT FUCKING GUN!"

"You ain't strong enough, boy!" Pauly whacked him upside the head with his fist, knocking something in his head loose. He went fuzzy and rolled right off Pauly, leaning against the bar in a daze.

Working his hands lower on the shotgun, his

fingers slipping around the heavy walnut stock, he reached back and swung out, clipping Stanley on the side of the head with the barrels.

Stanley muttered some gibberish and passed out cold.

Maxine cried out. "Get up Stanley!"

Dianne retreated back to her spot, thinking this was it. There was a madman out in the lanes, and in the bar she was trapped with whatever Pauly had become in a flash. She prayed and prayed that she would get out of here alive, that maybe Pauly would somehow succumb to the wound on his head, but he looked alive and full of vitality. She couldn't imagine how, because the wound had cracked open his head a slice, blood continued to pour from him in slick streams.

On his feet now, poking Stanley with the barrels, Pauly goaded him. "Wake up little boy, it's time for your medicine."

Stanley was coming back, slowly and drearily. His world distorted and gummy looking. His breathing was still a chore, and now he felt like he was suffocating, but then he realized why. Pauly shoved the barrel in his mouth hard enough to break teeth. "GET UP!"

Stanley's eyes rolled around, still trying to make sense of what was transpiring around him.

"I SAID GET UP GODDAMNIT!" Pulling the barrel from Stanley's mouth, he placed it over his kneecaps. "What's the matter, your legs don't work?"

Just then he jerked the trigger, a loud booming crack was swallowed in the room, taking Stanley's left leg off at the knee. Blood and pieces of bone punched into the carpet.

Allen screamed beneath a pool table, his hands over his ears, not wanting to hear Stanley out there moaning and rolling around. He had seen enough, but something inside himself told him to look, to watch what would happen next.

Maxine was screaming somewhere in the dark, and she knew she had to act fast, or else Pauly would get that light in his hands, put it on his next victim, and from then on, none of them would stand a chance.

Stanley was rocking back and forth, reaching for a leg that wasn't there. The natural movement in his limb was all wrong, the stump rising and falling pathetically, blood jetting in ribbons.

"Whoa! Now that's *allot* of blood, must have hit something important in there, huh?"

Swinging the barrels over his face, "Now let me help you with that breathing problem you got going on."

As he went to squeeze the trigger, a thick bottle fell over his skull, dropping him like a sack of pins to the ground.

CHAPTER 13

The rain just would not let up. It clashed with the speed of his windshield wipers, working over-time, cutting a path that just wouldn't hold. It was getting to the point where all this driving around was becoming a useless endeavor. And now with the streetlights and traffic signals all but wiped out due to a power failure, it was becoming more dangerous.

I can't see a goddamn thing out here.

The storm was dumping volumes of water over the area. Lightning strikes stabbed around the town, thunder continued vibrating through the chassis of the cruiser. And the wind, it swept over the vehicle like mad spirits howling into the night.

Sheriff McCarthy had given up on the radio after too many attempts that left him with nothing but white static to speak with. He stopped by the station after a quick patrol of the area showed no signs of Warner.

Once inside, he spoke with Maggy Cohen, she told him how she'd been working the phones and radio with no results, then the lights went out. After that, all they had working for them were the local stations. McCarthy told her to keep trying, maybe she'd pick up the right frequency. As she went about doing her thing under a pool of candle-light, McCarthy helped himself to the armory.

Inside were an assortment of rifles long sitting useless and collecting dust in the cabinet. There was a couple of decommissioned M-16s given to his department by the army a while back. After fixing them up with new firing pins and bolts, both of the weapons were certified and ready for service. He grabbed one, took a couple of 20 round box magazines, thinking about how good it would feel to put a few of these 5.56 slugs into that ugly mug of that night stalker out there. Now he just needed to find that man, show him what happens when you trespass on his land.

Where are you, you ugly sonofabitch…

Where indeed. He was hoping his deputies were having better luck than himself.

He decided on swinging back towards where the latest bodies had been found.

He parked on the curb, engine idling, near where flappy-face was found, the one whose head had been ripped apart by the curb, from the looks of it. Looking over to the passenger seat, the box of donuts was getting low. There was one left amidst a scattering of crumbs, a maple twist. He grabbed it, deep throated the thing, tore off a big bite, chewed and swallowed the rest.

Then a thought hit him as he stared out past the sweeping blinds. There were cars out there in the lot of the bowling alley, dark and shadowed beneath the storm. *What are they doing there so late?* He checked his watch. *11:23pm.* He took another bite of the donut, finishing it. *Silverside crew ought to be home by now.*

He shifted to drive, and rolled away from the curb, swinging right, descending the slope, he pulled into the Silverside Lanes lot, running his spotlight over the vehicles.

Empty, obviously. He drifted slowly around the rear of the building, nothing peculiar stuck out to him, just more rain lashing the windscreen and lightning licking the land.

Moving around up front, his spotlight hit the entry, and immediately, he froze. The glass surrounding that awful mural was cracked out of its frame, and more pertinent was the chain bundled around the handles.

Warner!

It had to be. He tried for the radio again, beating the hell out of the thing with his fist. "This is McCarthy, I need backup over at the lanes, over!"

Growing impatient, he punched the black box again, tried a few channels, and after a few twists and turns, he heard a voice break through the static. *'...orner of 4th.'*

"What the hell."

He swung the dial around until he could find that voice again. *Where'd you go, where'd you go now*, he mumbled to himself. Then it came through.

It was Miller, he would recognize that mans voice anywhere. A deep booming baritone of a voice. "Miller, this is McCarthy, I need everybody down at Silverside Lanes, pronto—how copy?"

Static followed, then eventually a voice; Miller's voice came in thick and loud. "Copy, sheriff, I'm en-route, over."

After a few more struggling moments with the radio, he managed to pull Stevens, Clyde, and Jefferson through to his location which required an effort that only put some more red in his big round rough face. He just hoped his other men would get the message in time.

Charles Warner saw something outside, moving in the parking lot. Now a car pulled close to the curb, a spotlight tossed a beam into the lanes, throwing shadows over the walls and floor. It was a police car, and Warner didn't like the police; he wasn't in the mood to be shackled again, placed under control, contained and removed from the hunt. There were still a handful of people to kill, and he wasn't about to let anyone get in his way. He had to think, which was difficult at times, because all he could ever think about was blood and pain. He was a savage, something loose from a worm hole of another time—another age. Warner had a simple outlook in life, and all it involved was breaking bodies and spilling blood; that's all there was to his life—nothing else existed outside that, no burdensome morality to stifle his lust.

The car door squeaked open, a man started rising out, his head was covered by a wide brim hat, his body was a shadow. Warner growled in his throat as he scowled at the man who could only have bad intentions for himself. He submerged in the shadows of the building, watching and waiting.

McCarthy had the spotlight glowing at the door. He welcomed the extra light after the power failure. He popped the trunk, grabbing the M16, stuffing the extra mag in his back pocket. Slamming the trunk, holding the rifle out, a flashlight in his other hand. He approached cautiously. Peering in through the shattered doors, he couldn't see much of anything, just a whole lot of crawling shadows and darkness.

He was thinking about calling out, but first he wanted that door open.

Snapping off the carabiner, he pulled the chain loose, dumping it on the steps behind him.

Using his boot, he pushed the door inside, and immediately his own flashlight showed him the headless man lying in a wide wet pool of his own blood. "Oh, Jesus Christ."

He immediately swung the rifle to the left, towards the lanes, thinking he'd seen something out of the corner of his eyes, but there was nothing there, just more of those long shadows. Sweeping the light around, not seeing much of anything else besides the grim looking corpse near the arcade machines, he moved in hesitantly, thinking maybe he should wait for Miller, Clyde, and Jefferson, but right then, he dismissed his own advice. *Don't be a hero, McCarthy, your almost 60 years old now, might not be good thing to go wandering in here any further, best just wait on your deputies.*

Maybe he should have, but the way he was seeing it was that he had already pushed into the building, he had an M16, selector switch on automatic, what could Warner do to him? If Warner was still here that is.

He decided to announce himself. "This is sheriff Dwight McCarthy of the Silverside Sheriff's department, I'm here to help, is anybody alive in the building?"

There were voices coming from the bar up on the right. He knew the place well, tossed back drinks with the bar keep many times. Pauly, a good man. His wife was a bit of trouble on him, but he never put that against him. "Pauly, you in there? This is McCarthy!"

The voices were low, muffled, as though trying their best to keep their presence a secret. "I hear you in there, this is sheriff McCarthy!"

He swung the light over the oval windows in the doors, and nearly shit himself when the chalky white face of a woman pressed against it. "Jesus— who is that?"

The voice was muffled behind the glass, but he could hear her all the same, said her name was Maxy or something.

McCarthy looked behind him, making sure something wasn't creeping up on him in the dark, then he got a look at that headless body again and it put a shiver up his spine. He pulled at the handles. "It's locked."

"Just a minute," she said. "We're barricaded."

He looked behind him as she went about clearing a path. He could hear what sounded like things sliding against the door. His light stabbed over the lanes, his rifle out ahead of him, watching the shadows. The place was dark as a tomb, the storm making it all that more terrible to go wandering around.

He noticed a bowling ball scratched up, *probably what shattered that door over there*. He swung the beam to the right, saw a few shoes thrown around. *Did they really think throwing shoes was going to do something? These people must have been scared out of their minds*. He could imagine. Seeing that man out there, it would do something to you.

The door swung open behind him with a gust of warm air, and another smell. A metallic odor hit him in the face. Death. It had to be.

"Please help us, please!"

He saw the girls eyes and he'd seen that look before. It was one of those looks only a hunted man could have, or one who had seen something too awful to speak about. He was guessing both of these were likely the case.

"It's okay now, ma'am." His light bled into the room. There were two other people standing near the pool tables, both shivering. A woman, a red-head, he recognized her, seen her around from time to time...*Dianna, Dianne!* That was it. She was the one who lost a husband to cancer. And the younger man, he'd seen him a few times cleaning the restroom, not much else. Then—

He saw the body of— "Is that Swallecki? Peter Swallecki?" He would recognize that fat sonofabitch anywhere. He remembers chasing him away from around Meyer Elementary a few times in the past. He knew about him, about those records he had stacked on his record.

"Yes..." She looked over, saw the mess. "Pauly killed him."

McCarthy paused before he spoke. "*Pauly?* Bartender Pauly? *Killed* Swallecki?"

She nodded her head.

"What in the ever loving hell for?"

She shook her head.

"Where's Pauly now?"

Her eyes fell to the ground, near a round table a few feet away, tucked in the shadows.

McCarthy swung his light. "He dead, too?"

"No, I hit him with a bottle, he's knocked out, I think..."

The sheriff lowered himself over Pauly, ran his light over the body. He saw the gash opened on his head, thought instantly the man was dead.

Placing two fingers on Pauly's neck, he came out of the squat. "Man's dead."

"Wha—I...I didn't mean to—I wasn—"

McCarthy could hear the pain, the regret, the horror. "It's alright, Maxy, don't let it worry you right now, just calm yourself, take a few breaths."

Her face fell in her hands.

"The boy outside," McCarthy was referring to the headless corpse. "Pauly do that to him, too?"

Her arms locked around her bosom now, shaking her head. "No, that was...the *other* man. The one with the scars on his face... Pauly, he thought it was that killer from the news."

He hadn't realized he had his back to the doors this whole time. And now feeling the hairs rise on his neck, he swung around, aiming both beam and rifle towards the doors. "He still here?"

"Yes, we...I mean...we think so."

McCarthy looked at the two shaking near the pool tables again. "Dianne right?"

She nodded her head. "Yes, yes, sheriff."

"You okay, sweetheart?"

She just shook her head.

"How about you fella? You hanging in there?"

He could see it in his eyes, that boy was scrambled, something inside his mind had gone black. The boy was sure to need help for the foreseeable future, that much was evident.

There was a moan coming from near the bar, just past Swallecki's headless body.

McCarthy put his light on it. "What the hell happened to him?"

As if she'd forgot about Stanley, Maxine's eyes jumped in their sockets. "That's Stanley. He was wrestling the gun from Pauly, when Pauly hit him in the head, then..." She looked like she couldn't finish.

"Then Pauly took his leg off with that shotgun you have leaning up behind you?"

She looked behind her nervously. "I—I'm afraid sheriff."

"I imagine you're all pretty shook up."

He leaned over Stanley, noticed the blood in his mouth, the gaps along his gums, his leg pulped in shredded bloody meat. "It's going to be alright partner, I'll have the ambulance here in no time." It was a lie, but better to give the man some hope.

Swinging the light around, thinking maybe there were more than the four of them in here somewhere. "Anybody else here?"

Maxine bit her lip. "There were...more of us. Hardy—"

"The grease monkey?" McCarthy interrupted, knowing all too well about his run-ins with that metal head.

"...Yes. And my friend...*Joanne*." Saying that name was more painful than she imagined. She felt a piece of her—a very vital piece inside of her—go to jelly; a spike of pain twisted in her belly just thinking about her friend...her bloody head spinning in the tray out there.

"Anybody else?" McCarthy asked.

She shook her head.

"Okay..." he looked around, trying to get his bearings on the situation. He was alone, just the four of them, and moving the young man out without a leg was going to be one bitch of a task. So that option was looking unlikely. He had a woman with a thousand yard stare going on, mumbling things about her friend Joanne, and how she didn't mean to kill Pauly, it was truly heartbreaking for him to hear it. Then there was Dianne who looked like a walking corpse, and that young fella, Allen, he thought he heard somebody say earlier. The boy looked wound tight as a live wire. One wrong move and that kid would jump from his skin. He had a very delicate situation to deal with, and the possibility that Warner was still inside, maybe even watching them now, from outside those doors, somewhere in the shadows.

"You know how to use that thing?" McCarthy asked, pointing to the double barrel.

She hesitated a moment. "Yes, I…I just don't know how to load it. It only has one shot, I think."

He came around, set his rifle down on the table, took the shotgun in his hands. Pushing the lever aside on the top, the breach popped open. He grabbed at the empty, tossing it. "Any extras around here?"

She pointed to Pauly. "In his pocket, the top pocket on his shirt."

McCarthy handed her the gun. He went over to Pauly's body, rolled him over, felt over his pockets and brought out two extra shells.

Taking the gun from her, he slotted in the fresh shell. "See how I went about that?"

She nodded.

"Good, here's an extra shell. Right now you have two shots. Both these here," he pointed to the rabbit ears. "You just thumb these back, and these," pointing to the double triggers. "Just a little bit of pressure to blow one shell, hold it hard, and both shells fly, but the recoil will be a real bitch, you understand?"

She nodded again.

He offered her the shotgun, grabbing up his M16.

"Okay," he swung the light over the frightened faces. "I'm going out there, I need to find this man, soon as I leave these doors, you all help and barricade this place back up." They looked bereaved already, like he was abandoning them all. "Don't worry none, I have back up arriving shortly. And you can be sure we'll find this man."

"Maxy,"

"It's *Maxine*..." she managed to say.

"Good, Maxine—you keep that shotgun handy, you see a face with scars on it, you give him both barrels, understand?"

"Yes, sir..." she whispered.

"Okay then."

He started forward, poking his light out into the lanes, scattering some shadows around, creating others. His neck bobbed with a swallow. "If anything happens to me, you all wait here, help is coming."

Turning, stepping outside the door, something

165

big obstructed his way, a wall of some kind, and it was breathing down on him.

"Oh Jesus H Christ!"

The bowling pin came quick. Warner jammed the slim end into McCarthy's mouth, using his palm to shove it down deep, but the girth of the pin was preventing such easy access, so instead, Warner had to get creative.

With the pin lodged in his mouth, all he could do was squirm around at the pain. He dropped the rifle, hands reaching up, trying to remove the thick pin from his throat, but Warner wasn't having that.

With his fingers plugged into the sheriff's mouth, on either side of the pin, with little effort, he pulled and tore McCarthy's cheeks apart in bloody wet flaps. Now with more room to work with, Warner set his palm on the back end of the pin and pushed and pushed, and pushed some more, until the pin was now sticking half out his ragged mouth.

Blood flew up and around the pin.

Dianne screamed, running further back into the bar, finding a spot she was hoping she wouldn't be found.

Allen tossed his stomach up again, on his knees now, choking out whatever he could. He fell to his side in a paralyzed shock.

Maxine grabbed the shotgun, her eyes blown wide in their sockets, blood going from her face at the horror of what that man was doing to the sheriff.

McCarthy was gagging on his own blood, the pin was now an obscene cork that plugged his mouth, only a few inches poke from around his lips. Warner pushed the sheriff to the ground, stepping on his chest until a popping crack ran over his body, breaking old bones, he stepped into the room, blood all over his face.

Maxine screamed, raised the shotgun and blew off a shot, but the power behind it made the shot wildy erratic, it tore a hole in the ceiling, plaster clouded over Warner. She raised the gun again, squeezed off a shot, a roiling cloud of flame belched out the end, and this time, she landed a hit, a bad hit that had him limping out of there, but she knew it wasn't over. She hurriedly reloaded the shotgun, breaking it open just as the sheriff had showed her only moments ago. She ejected both red casings, inserting the last. Snapping it closed, she moved forward. There was movement somewhere out in the lanes, but she couldn't see anything. Lightning tossed a blue flare and she saw him, limping out towards the warehouse.

Running back inside the bar. "Dianne, Allen, grab Stanley, LET'S GO!"

Allen started crawling towards her. "Dianne, where are you? Damnit!"

She looked at Allen. "Where's Dianne?"

He was sobbing and moaning too bad to speak.

She grabbed up the flashlight on the ground. She swung the light around. "DIANNE!?" The light hit a flicker of something on the pool table. *The knife.* She ran forward, grabbed it, shoved it carefully in her back pocket. "DIANNE!?"

"SHIT!"

She helped Allen to his feet. "Come on, Allen, you have to help me grab Stanley—Get up!"

"I can't do it!" He was trying, oh was he trying, but everything was happening too quick. There was so much he had seen, and none of it was pretty. He wasn't built for this, but who was? He was a recluse mostly, except when hanging with Jeremy, his best friend, who was now out there, lying headless in a pool of his own blood. He didn't want to see anymore. He wanted to get home, crawl in bed, watch things to make him feel human again. So he lifted himself to his feet, taking Maxine's hand.

She put the light on him. "You see where Dianne went?"

He just shook his head, moaning and muttering like a mute.

"SHIT!"

She went to Stanley who instantly swatted her hand away. "Don't waste your time," he croaked. "Get out while you can, I'm done...I've...lost allot of blood..."

"No, Stanley, we're getting you out of here— Allen! Help me over here!"

But she might as well have been speaking to a cardboard cutout. "GODDAMNIT ALLEN!!"

Lowering into a crouch, trying to get an arm

under him, Stanley just pushed her away again. "I said GO! Get out of here Max, don't worry..."

She stood, tears running down her face. "We'll get help, Stanley—I promise!"

Maxine took Allen by the wrist, pulling him towards the door like a child. She stepped out first, near the arcades now, followed by a staggering Allen. Then, a grunt came from behind her, followed by a spray of something hot and wet that splashed over her neck.

She looked behind her, Allen had a pry bar in his neck, Warner was standing behind him, his scars pulled up in a terrible grin.

She lost it right then. The shotgun went out, and the whole thing was in slow motion as he jerked the trigger, the buckshot punched a bowling ball crater in Allen's chest.

His eyes locked on her own in a shock of surprise.

Blood welled up in his sockets, pouring down his eyes. The end of the bar poking from his neck had a fist of meat on it. The hole in his chest was gushing blood and other things, dark things, wet things, coiling loopy things. His ribs jutted out like somebody had ripped them out, left them pried open.

Warned pushed the boy from the bar where he slid forward, dropping hard on his knees. He brought the bar up to his lips, licked up the blood that sat slicked and thick as syrup along the length.

Maxine let the shotgun fall from her hands, not wanting to use it anymore, she shuddered in revulsion, in fear, in horror—hatred.

His grin widened showing a set of crooked yellow teeth that grew at odd angles. His black eyes, deep as gunshot wounds.

Maxine screamed.

Warner started after her, licking the blood from his lips.

She took a few steps back and felt gravity loosen up as she went smacking onto the ground in a pool of warm blood.

Jeremy.

Her heels caught in the slimy sea of red, she fought to gain balance, to get herself out of there.

Warner was only a few feet away when a shadow rose up behind him. It was Dianne, she had something in her hands. It was a pool stick.

She screamed out. "NNNNOOOO!!!" With whatever strength she could summon, she swung the long piece of lumber, cracking it right over Warner's skull. But the damage, if there was any to speak of, was short lived. Because right then, he swiveled, coming around with a thick meaty fist and catching her with a bone whacking smack upside the head. Her eyes grew wide, she buckled, folded up like wet laundry and smacked face first into Allen's corpse.

Maxine found some traction, using it, she righted herself. Standing, she felt the blade in her pocket, it was all she had now. She went to grab it, when she screamed instead.

Warner was lowering over Dianne, smelling at her from the looks of it. Even with the little bit of light tossed in the place from the glaring spotlight out front, she could see his nostrils flaring, it was a disturbing image.

She swallowed as she slowly went for the knife, afraid to make any sudden motions, it was like backing out of a dark cave when the bear was feeding.

Then he did something that caused her to shriek out in a muffled cry.

He took that bar and stuck it down her throat, working it like a plunger. She came alive with the pain, jolting straight up, trying to scream, but it came out in a bubbling foam of blood that boiled from her mouth. Warner was enjoying it, Maxine knew, because each thrust brought a delighted sort of depravity to moan from his throat. It was almost sexual sounding, and it caused her to wretch up whatever she could.

Working the pry bar faster and faster as his excitement increased, he was tearing a ragged line in her neck from the friction. It was opening up, spilling blood out of her throat, gushing like a broken main, flooding over Allen's body below.

Tearing the bar free, he placed the chiseled flat edge beneath her eye and shoved it inside, scooping out the orb. It was surprising she was still alive. Or was she? Maxine couldn't be sure, but her body responded as if it were, though it could have been a billion nerves firing at once. It was like someone stuck a live wire in her ass. Her legs kicked out, the backs of her hands sweeping through the blood around her. She was jolted by rippling spasms. Removing the bar, he did the same to her other eye, but left the bar inside of her. He started rotating the handle like a crank, scrambling her brain like porridge.

Maxine had enough.

She turned to run, when several shadows appeared by the entrance.

They were screaming at her, but she wasn't hearing it. She screamed right back at those shadows and hauled herself down the steps, running, going for the warehouse. Once inside, she twisted the lock and waited.

CHAPTER 14

Immediately there were a series of gunshots, not just a few, but what sounded to be numerous different calibers hammering away; following that, were voices, loud screaming; shouting voices of command, authority. But after a time, some of those voices sounded weak, and whinny, like scared little boys running from some junkyard dog. Then a high shrilling scream like someone had stepped in a bear trap and couldn't get loose. And like that, the scream cut off, and the gunshots, they were just an echo.

Maxine heard all of this, thinking—hoping—they had gotten him. He was dead. He had to be dead. The man wasn't immune to gunfire, was he? It seemed like no matter what, he just wouldn't stop coming. Like some sort of machine sent from the future, it was a terrible thought.

She shot him herself, with that big shotgun Pauly had used to kill Swallecki with. But how bad was it? *Couldn't have been too bad for him to come in here where your hiding now, grab a pry bar, run back out front, and kill Allen, then Dianne with the same tool, now could it?* In fact, she hadn't even remembered him limping after coming back. Was it all in her head? It mattered none, she supposed.

The guy out there, whatever he is, whomever he is—*could it really be that man from the massacre? like Pauly was whispering about*—he was uncanny and brutal. He was the real boogieman, the night haunter, the ripper, the campground slayer, whichever way you look at it, that man was a *nightmare*. And just like any nightmare, he kept coming back, and with a new twist at each turn.

She held the knife in her hand, her chest rising and falling rapidly. Her black hair lay frayed and slicked in blood. Jeremy's blood, maybe Allen's blood, too; come to think of it, she probably had a little bit of everybody's blood on her right about then.

A gunshot brought her back.

She froze up, then another gunshot—

Then a scream, a high pitched squealing.

She could hear the tell tale sounds of boots running over hard ground and knew somebody was on the lanes.

Another gun shot caused a jolt to issue from her.

She couldn't see a damn thing. Only blackness; sheets of ebon shadows, a night scape.

Another scream, one that just wouldn't end, it seemed to drag on and on until it, too, like the other few, had just cut off—unplugged and dead.

Squeeeeek

The door to the warehouse had opened. The sound was obvious, she'd heard it a thousand times, and for some strange reason she wondered why Hardy had never hit it with that WD40 he had plenty of lying around here. It was a fleeting thought, like her brain trying to remember things that weren't wrapped around horror, bring her back to a sanity unlike what she was physically experiencing at the moment.

There were footsteps, loud and menacing lurking in the dark.

For one insane moment, she thought she saw that man out there, but he didn't look like a man anymore, but something that couldn't be real. What she was seeing was something with burning neon-red eyes that scanned the room. A mechanical stride to his limbs. In her mind, she saw the thing had a knife in his hands like something out of one of those Frank Frazetta paintings, long as an arm, wickedly curved, sharp as hammer forged steel. It was gleaming off those red eyes, and suddenly, it found her.

She felt the clamping strength of its fingers curl around her wrists, then a wash of cold dark air whipped over her as she was hauled crudely to her feet.

The knife was no longer there, and those eyes, both gone, replaced with two shiny black orbs that poked out at her from the dark.

His lips slid back and those big crooked yellow teeth were on show, like neon, pushing right into the dark.

She screamed as he released one hand and ran

his big thick fingers over her face, as if he were examining her, getting a feel for her. One finger slid over her lips, then forced itself in her mouth.

She gagged and coughed, he slapped her.

There was something in her hand, then she remembered.

The knife!

Her eyes went wide in the dark, her grimace, a snarling mad beast as she lashed out, and opened a long slant over the scars on his face.

Warner reeled back, sinking further into the shadows.

He was groaning.

Maxine swung out in the dark, thinking he was still here, but his voice was being carried around the place, far off, yet near. She couldn't be sure. What mattered was razing his face again, or, better yet, his throat!

She took a few steps forward, using her toes to probe ahead. Her arm sprung out, after catching a glimpse of those evil red eyes that she knew weren't there, but in her mind, they were as clear as crystal. The knife cut air and nothing more.

She moved on.

Behind her, she sensed movement.

Abruptly, she swiveled, came in low and stabbed out and screamed, thinking for sure he was there and that knife would find flesh. But only empty space.

Maxine was hyper, her body alert and stressed. Aware of every minute sound around the place, she could hear a mouse sneeze at that moment. And speaking of movement, there was plenty of it. She was hearing breathing and the shuffling of feet over pavement. *Where is he, Max, WHERE IS HE!?*

God, how she wanted to scream, scream and just run away, into the night. Maybe dig a hole out in that field in the back, hide forever away from this nightmare.

Then closer movement brought her back, like tools falling and nuts and bolts spilling from jars.

Her hip ran into something and she nearly screamed.

She swung out again, thinking that was him. The one with red eyes, and sometimes black.

But again, she only sliced away the darkness.

Something was sticky under her feet now, like walking through glue. She used her other hand, sweeping ahead of her until—

Her fingers felt something vaguely familiar. She felt further, and then the tips of her fingers sank into a mire of something warm and wet.

She brought her fingers up to her nose and took a whiff. It was blood. The unmistakable aroma of wet metal. This time she did scream. And when she did, her foot caught something and she went down on her back.

Warner homed in like a hot beacon.

He was on her now.

She was screaming and swinging out with that blade. "GET OFF GET OFF GET OFF GETOFFGET-OFFGETOFF!!!"

She punctuated each word with that blade, she could feel its short length cutting flesh, and each time it did, Warner squirmed and grunted, groaned and croaked.

Then, yes, the flicker of lights opened up overhead. Her irises fought the harsh florescence of the lighting popping to life.

Warner lay on top of her, he was heavy, but not only that, he was still moving. And now she witnessed the damage she inflicted. His face lay in flaps, the skull beneath partially exposed. One eye had been slit open and was bursting out juicing liquids that fell into her face, trailing like slug slime. She turned her head at the revolting taste and feel of it oozing on her. Then, he came alive in a thrashing move, like an alligator, twisting and spasming over a piece of fresh meat.

He howled in her face, and it was a hot fetid odor that sank into her pores.

She screamed. "FUCK YOU!!!"

She swung the blade again, the tip cutting across his other eye. His torso lifted free from her. The pulp of his eye drained down his face, past the bloody flaps that hung like peeled wallpaper. Then he looked down at her, and she screamed a nightmare of a shriek that brought that terrible grin of his to the light; his hands found her neck and he squeezed.

She was choking and doing her best not to drop the knife.

Her vision was blurry and indistinct as if fading to sleep. With effort, she swung out again, and again. The blade opened trenches of blood along his face and neck, across his eyeless sockets. Blood showered over her, dusting her face, squirting out at her.

Then her fist tightened, and like a hammer strike, she came forward and down, and the blade, all four inches, sank its bloody length into his neck.

His hands released her neck, but he continued to straddle her.

Reaching up, he grabbed at the handle, felt the blood pumping around the wound. He looked down at her again with that grin, and a deranged laughter came bubbling out of his throat. Her own lips squirmed and sucked into her mouth thinking this was it, she was dead now. He was going to remove that knife and pepper her face full of holes and openings. She was preparing for the pain—the agony. Then—

He continued to laugh that horrible, beastly snorting laughter.

And to her shocked surprise, he drew the blade across his neck like a zipper and a hot fountain of crimson fell over her face like a cracked dam.

And through the sheets of red blinding over her, he reached back, the little knife raised above him, and if he had eyes, she would imagine the both of them being insanely wide—

Gunshots, a wall of led, shells casings and booming echoes.

Her eyes fluttered at the blood blossoming and geysering from the holes opening in his chest like little eyes—cherry blood-red eyes.

The knife fell behind him as his body went rigid. Then, like a granite slab of a tomb struck by a bolt of lightning, he toppled.

Deputy Travis Miller was the first one in the door.

He shouted at the lady in the black hair and wild eyes. She looked frightened to the point of incapacitation. She was flecked in blood and deranged. As he screamed for her to duck, she ran instead, disappearing deep in the shadows.

That's when he and Stevens, Clyde, and Jefferson, saw the man in there, covered in dark stains, his face twisted and ridged in bumping scars of pink that were now channeled in blood.

Warner.

Miller then wondered where in the hell McCarthy had gotten off, too. His car was outside, but there was no sign of their sheriff.

He explicitly told them each not to go off and become like that buff actor, Arnold...something or other, and act like a commando. Told them all to wait for one another. But, he knew McCarthy well, and his brazen ways got the best of him even in the worst possible circumstances. He was sure the sheriff was inside somewhere, most likely dead, too.

Then he saw it.

The sheriffs boots were sticking from a door on the right. He recognized the tan slacks immediately. And Miller's rage went through the roof right then.

"Open fire!!"

They wasted no time.

Guns opened up, smoking trails of led blowing into the dark, shell casings flicking off the pavement.

They pushed inside, keeping the line tight, avoiding a catastrophe that could end very bad if anybody got ahead, accidentally clipping your own teammate wasn't something any of them wanted to deal with.

The bullets continued to pop and spark off things in the building.

But, where in the hell did that big ugly monster get to?

"HOLD FIRE!!!"

A few shots petered out, then silence.

Flashlights came on, running over where they had seen Warner. But where was he?

There was blood dotting around, and, Jesus, a headless body, a young man from the looks of it. But where the hell was his head.

"Found something," Clyde said.

The three of them moved closer to Clyde.

"Holy shit."

It was all they could say, if they could say anything at all. Blood, and lots of it, and bodies...and the sheriff, something only a demon was capable of.

McCarthy was right, Miller got to thinking. This was no man, but a beast, a monster. Men don't do things like this. Not sane ones anyhow. This man took his time, experimented.

There was no time to look over the macabre sculpture of their sheriff. Now was a time to find that evil man, hunt him down, finish what McCarthy intended.

"Spread out, but keep it tight," Miller advised.

Light beams bobbed and swayed, breaking apart the darkness.

It took only a moment for the horror show to kick off. And victim number one was screaming.

It was Stevens.

His light fell to the floor beneath him. A shadow had him by the neck. Then Stevens made a wet gurgling sound after Warner grabbed the flailing arm that held the pistol. Stevens squeezed off a shot that drilled one of the scoreboard screens. Black glass exploded, dusting the lane below it. Warner grabbed the pistol, put it in that cop's mouth and helped the man pull the trigger again. Only this time instead of black glass exploding, there was a muffled thump, and a bowl of skull fragments blowing out behind him in a busted balloon of blood and brain cubes.

Warner let Stevens drop after that.

"YOU SONOFABITCH!!!" Clyde opened up on the shadow after that. Both hands wrapped securely around his 9mm. He couldn't see anything, but it didn't matter, what mattered was putting rounds where he saw Warner. Of course, that little act did nothing but flash his location to Warner, who was now off to the side, a bowling ball in his hands. He fast pitched it, the marbled surface smacking Clyde in the skull with a nasty popping echo.

Jefferson and Miller were throwing beams of light over the lanes, looking for the man, but they couldn't see him. "HE'S A GODDAMN GHOST!!"

"ENOUGH of that!" Miller told him.

"THEN WHERE THE FUCK IS HE!?!"

Miller couldn't answer that. He rushed over to Clyde.

Clyde looked back at him with frosted, glassy eyes.

He was dead.

His head split down the middle like a fault line. Blood was streaming into a pool, his brain was swelling through the cracks.

Jefferson ran past Miller after seeing the horror of Clyde's eyes.

"WHERE THE FUCK ARE YOU, HUH!? I'LL KILL YOU!! Jefferson, a normally calm man, a fatherly look to him, on account he had three youngins at home, was moving out on the lanes like a man possessed, swinging his .45 over the place, his flashlight secure in his grip. A hunter. A killer—a warrior. He needed Warner to show himself. "SHOW YOURSELF GODDAMNIT!!!"

Then he did.

He broke from the shadows. How he did it,

Jefferson hadn't time to ponder. But he blew off three booming shots that did little to put the breaks on Warner who came barreling over to him like a mack truck gone rogue.

Jefferson screamed, and continued to scream when Warner held him by the throat, then his other hand sank into his mouth, finding the deputies tongue, and giving it a nice tug, and more tugs until he heard that sweep ripping sound. He dropped Jefferson to the freshly polished lane after that, only now it was oiled in blood and was scuffed and scratched.

Holding the tongue out ahead of him in victory, Miller saw this and ordered him to stop.

Warner just grinned and came at him.

"I said stop and put your fucking hands up! Now!"

But Warner was unimpeded.

Miller's eyes grew wide as ping pong balls right then.

Then Warner tossed that length of bloody tongue over to Miller. It smacked him in the face.

Miller screamed in revulsion, dropping his gun, accidentally kicking it across the lanes where the shadows swallowed it up. He started to run away, when Warner got a hold of him, pulled him close.

Miller fought and scratched at the man, but nothing seemed to stop him. Then he got lucky, landing a foot in the man's nuts. It buckled him a moment.

He turned to run, made it a few steps of the

way. He looked for something in the low amount of lighting. Then—

He saw it.

An M16.

He dove for it, then Warner came out of the shadows again. Put a heavy boot on his wrist, breaking it like a light bulb.

Miller screamed, then another heavy boot hit him the face, then all went black.

He came alive from the screams shouting out from somewhere across the lanes.

The neon tubing of the place suddenly flickered and hummed, throwing pink and purple blooms over the place. It was a slaughterhouse. Bodies, blood, glass, smoke hanging thick as clouds from the gunfire.

Another scream.

Flashing his eyes, he used his hand to push himself up, but screamed as the bones were shattered in his left palm. He used his other hand, then to grab at the M16. He reached out for, taking it in his hand. Rolling on his back, he sat up, looked around, saw allot of blood and glass...*McCarthy, Jesus, sir*, and that headless boy, also... a female and another boy, both horribly massacred.

His rage put him on his feet.

There was laughter that sounded more like lunacy than mirth.

He started forward, something on the lanes caught his eyes.

Jefferson!

He was pulling himself forward like a dying dog.

Miller ran after him. "Jefferson..."

He rolled him over. Blood shot out of his mouth and nose. "Oh...*fuck*— Jefferson!" Jefferson just slumped after that, dying in his own blood. He'd probably choked on a gallon of the stuff.

Another scream caught his attention.

He looked to the left, saw a door.

Kicking it open, he ran inside.

A little ways in, he saw him, perched over that black haired female from earlier, blood was everywhere. Two more bodies, one missing its head.

He didn't bother saying anything.

With his good hand, he held the grip tight, bracing it with the back of his fractured hand. The gun bucked and vibrated as the concussive wave of rounds blew towards Warner. The bullets stitched him over the chest, drilled into his belly, blew out gouts of flesh and rosettes of blood. After the mag went dry, Warner toppled over on the woman.

She started screaming.

CHAPTER 15

"It's a massacre."

That's what they were saying. What more could you say in such a case? There were bodies everywhere. Blood smeared the lanes. A couple of headless bodies, brutally mauled victims, some crafty, medieval designs of tortured killings. It was all very savage—primal.

The state police showed up after Maggy Cohen had finally gotten through.

Deputy O'Donnell was helping her out on the radio, on account his own cruiser suffered a flat, and being only a few blocks from the station, he hiked his ass back, escaping the onslaught of rain that lashed at him like razorblades.

Eventually he made it out to the lanes, in his personal car, to assist the state authorities with the mop up and investigation.

The bodies were laid out on the wet pavement. White sheets draped over them, no longer white, but saturated and thick with blood. It was a good thing the storm had abated and moved on, almost like Warner had brought it with him, and when he died...

They found a man alive in the bar, lying next to the gutted body of a bigger man that had most of his head spread over the bar counter and bottles on the shelves.

His name was Stanley he told them. It was hard to tell if he were alive or dead, his face looked more like the latter. Like something that crawled out of an old grave. Ashen and gray. He died shortly after they put him on a stretcher.

A massive amount of blood loss they said.

Once they cleared the warehouse, a girl came screaming out of a corner at them. A knife in her hands. She had a crazy look in her eyes, and they almost put her down like a rabid animal, but hesitated when they noticed she had just gone mad, or at least had the look of one riven with madness—insanity.

They carefully walked her to the front where she was helped into a waiting ambulance. She saw Warner's body out there on the sidewalk, and like a cruel joke, the wind played with her. It blew his sheet over so she could see his face while sitting in the ambulance.

And if she weren't so certain he was dead, she would think she saw him grinning at her right then.

She screamed.

EPILOGUE

"NOOOO!!!" Her cries went unheard. Or more precisely, they echoed back to her in the vast chamber of steel pipes and machines that surrounded her. *Where the hell am I*, she wondered.

She felt a hot breeze play over her skin, she looked down and saw she was in a white gown, like one of those old Victorian get ups, but it was shredded, her breasts lay exposed—her nipples stiff. Blood ran down her face.

She screamed.

There was something there, just behind her, but she couldn't see it with all those billowing clouds of steam ringing around the piping and walkways that seemed endless. But then something came rolling forward. She looked closely, she recognized this, but from where?

A bowling ball, that's what it was. There were several now, coming out of the steam, and each one was trailing...*blood?* It sure looked like it. Streaks of crimson ran over the steel footing beneath her. She could hear it dripping and squishing, then the balls rolled by her, under her, around her, but never hitting her.

Now there was something else coming out of the hot mist. It looked like a ball. But—No, it was a... head. It had hair, but its face was terribly shredded, peeled, flayed to the bone. Blood shot out as it tumbled, then another one came rolling out, and another, until a whole wall of heads started pouring out of the mist. She screamed when she saw the face because, yes, she knew that face, it was her friend, the love of her life. It was Joanne. A grinning skull face of Joanne!

She ran, tripping over bloody heads, and then she fell on her face, blood covered her. Then...it was gone.

God it was hot—stifling really.

Where was she now? A long stretch of pipes and knobs, brass wheels and more of that mist opened up now. There was something shadowy in its depths. Her eyes narrowed, then...oh God, yes, it was a body. A big ragged hole in its chest. Something sticking from its throat, blood was running down its face...no, not its face. Allen's face! She cried out for him. "I DIDN'T MEANT IT I DIDN'T MEAN IT, NO NO NO!!!"

She turned and ran, blowing through the hot fog that wound over her.

She stepped in something, her feet sucked in a bog of some sorts. The hot mist receded, showing her a swamp, big black trees around her, branches hanging down, crooked and lifelike, reaching for her. She swatted and screamed at those branches. Then something came out of the bog, but it wasn't a bog anymore, but a swamp of blood, and in it were heads and bowling pins, balls floating as if they could float. Then whatever came out of the blood was on her now, crawling up her legs. It was a hand! Then another hand. Stanley! Yes, it was Stanley, he was pulling himself up to her, trying to drag her into the swamp with him. She fought him, kicked and tried to run, but she fell, sinking beneath the blood. Breaking the surface she gasped, spitting blood and other things she didn't want to think about.

But now...she found herself in an office. A brass name plate in big bold black letters said MR. SWALLECKI! She turned to run out of there, when something blocked her path. Headless and blowing out a torrent of black blood from his neck, Swallecki reached out for her. His fingers grubby and swollen, nails snapped off, the bones protruding. He was naked. His penis, like his fingers, had swelled to the size of an uncured salami log, it was rising and filling out. She kicked at it and swiveled, running...back into the machine world.

She took off down a long corridor of pipes and blood, bowling racks made up the walls, pins lay scattered. Rounding a corner, she hit a wall, fell down, then looked up and saw it wasn't no wall, but a man. Or...something with the anatomical skeleton of one anyhow. It was a machine. Gleaming alloy with....wait, the head...it was... *WARNER!* But...No, how! Then the eyes...black sockets that filled out with a burning red-neon. And he grinned, the flesh around his face falling off in wet bloody flaps. And his teeth were no longer yellow, but chrome and machine like, pointed even—like canines.

It reached out for her with long metallic fingers that ended with curving knife blades, then she screamed.

And the Warner machine liked it when she screamed. Because its eyes were glowing hot, the red blazing and building up into something volcanic.

She looked on in horror as those eyes boiled in colors and hues, then suddenly, two pinpoint lasers shot down towards her, searing—coring into her body, her skin bubbled over like soapy foam; then the heat took over and burned away her flesh like tallow and it ran from her bones in thick clods of bloody grease, then—

She awoke screaming, and screaming, but her hands and limbs afforded no movement. She took a moment to look around, but couldn't see much of anything except the white walls, and sterile smell. There was a window with a sheet of interlocking chain over it as a screen. Moonlight poured through the aperture. Sweat beaded her face, soaked through her clothes. There was a contraption, a cart of sorts, a computer monitor with a black screen, green lettering flashing over in some binary code.

She managed to look down at her self, saw the leather bindings holding her in place, could see her breasts poking through the thin white fabric. Wires ran over her like translucent veins. "NO! WHERE AM I!! HELP HELP!!!" Then she saw, between her feet, over on the wall out there, a big black window. Tinted, a two way.

A door flew open, a block of yellowish light behind it. Two figures rushed inside. A woman in a white smock, a big hulking man that looked more like Warner without the scars dressed in white pants and top.

She shrunk back into herself when he got close, as if she'd been through this before, and didn't want to experience it anymore. The woman moved up, cooing and saying things to her, like, "It's alright, dear, you're safe, no boogieman will get you, okay sweetie?"

But the boogieman, he was there in the room with her. And he had a needle in his hands. A thick canister of opaque liquid sat sloshing in the tube.

"NOOOO!!!"

"Hold her down, damnit!" the big man instructed.

The woman gritted her teeth and held Maxine down.

The needle poked rudely into her vein, then Maxine relaxed, her eyes going hazy and foggy.

She got a good look at the man with the needle, saw him grinning at her—

Her world went black.

The doctor walked in just then. His white coat billowing as if he were in haste. His thin glasses held to his face as though made just for him. His black hair lay slicked and immaculate. A gaunt face, youngish, green eyes framed with a pair of thin wire spectacles. "Is she ready?"

"Yes, doctor Grant," the big man said.

"Is the dose stronger this time?"

"Yes, doctor, Grant."

"Good, because I need her to sleep longer, it's the only way I can test my theory."

"But...but doctor," the petite nurse stammered. "Why make her relive this every night, every day! It was three years ago! What help have you given her!? Why, doctor!? What insane theory are you attempting to prove?!"

"*DON'T* question me!"

"But..."

"Enough!" The doctor moved in real close. "Now, I'm not going to have any trouble with you, too, am I, nurse Anna?

Nurse Anna looked scared, terrified really. Those gleaming green eyes of his had a note of evil swimming in the irises. She knew of the bodies, heard about that building across the grounds—the old sanitarium that was shut down years before. There were rumors he had lobotomy patients out there, lost in those walls, others strapped to wire beds. Even more disturbing rumors of a great pit full of failed experiments, which in this case were patients, rotting and mouldering. Why he wanted this Maxine girl to relive her nightmare, her grief and torment, over and over—an endless infernal hell—she hadn't a clue, but knew enough not to ever rise so sharply, lest she be added to the pit.

"No...no, doctor."

"Good." Turning to the big man. "Now give her the shot."

"Yes, doctor Grant."

The big man moved forward, pulling another shot from his coat, sinking the syringe. The nurse got a look at the new shot. Her eyes widened, *But she'll never wake up! You'll put her in a coma, then she'll live with this forever!* That's what she wanted to say, if she possessed the courage to do so. But, again, she knew it unwise to speak up.

His lips curled in an evil sneer as the plunger squeezed out the liquid. He moved over to Maxine, stroked her sweaty black hair. In a sonorous voice, he said "Rest my child. Warner is waiting."

Anna ran from the room, followed by the doctors incessant cackling.

A storm had opened up over the grounds, lashing winds threatening the trees ringed in the courtyard. Lightning stabbed the building.

And inside the corridors of Hollow Falls Sanitarium, Maxine Macy silently slipped into eternal rest.

AFTERWORD

Thank you for reading the latest in the
Slasherback Series. I really enjoyed writing
this one. This one was born out of a few of my
favorites such as Intruder (1989) The Mutilator
(1984) a bit of Silent Night, Deadly Night
(1984) even a dusting of The Dead Pit (1989).
I'm already fast typing away at the third in
the series, and hope to have it out soon! Also,
I have something special planned in time for
Halloween! Until then, keep reading horror.

Brian G. Berry

Printed in Great Britain
by Amazon

17251891R00115